A Cageful

By the same author

The Strollers

A Cageful of Butterflies

LESLEY BEAKE

RED FOX

A Red Fox Book

Published by Random House Children's Books
20 Vauxhall Bridge Road, London SW1V 2SA

A division of Random House UK Ltd
London Melbourne Sydney Auckland
Johannesburg and agencies throughout the world

Copyright © Lesley Beake 1989

1 3 5 7 9 10 8 6 4 2

First published by
Maskew Miller Longman (Pty) Ltd, Cape Town 1989

Published simultaneously in Great Britain
in hardback and paperback by
The Bodley Head Children's Books and Red Fox 1995

Phototypeset by Intype, London
Printed and bound in Great Britain by
Cox & Wyman Ltd, Reading, Berkshire

RANDOM HOUSE UK Limited Reg. No. 954009

Papers used by Random House UK Limited
are natural, recyclable products made from wood grown in
sustainable forests. The manufacturing processes conform to
the environmental regulations of the country of origin

ISBN 0 09 929581 4

To my friends Em and Ray

Mponyane was real. He lived and died in Northern Natal fifteen years ago. He couldn't hear and he couldn't speak, but he gave.

Before

Before, there was a *kraal*[1] in the mountains of northern Natal, where the frost lay white in the winter and the sun dreamed slow in the summer. Mubi, who had his name because he was so very ugly (and Mubi means very ugly man), was grandfather, and father, to a family here. In the beginning it was good and the *mealies*[2] grew high and green, but then came the time of no rain when the young men left to find work in the cities, because there was not enough food. Some of them did not come back, and Mubi's son was one of these, but he left behind a grandson for Mubi; a boy called Mponyane, whom the old man loved.

Before, there was a village in the valley, where the black dust from the coal blew in at every crack in the windows and the men were grey from the workings when they came up to the light once again. Here there lived a woman who knew much trouble and whose own people had turned against her, with hate in their minds. She had no man to protect her, but two children, who brought strength to her heart; a boy whose name was Frank, and a girl called Cecily. The woman's friend was the old man, Mubi, the very ugly man. He was her friend because once she had

[1.] enclosure
[2.] corn

1

turned away from her people and their ways, and had found wisdom in the *kraal* in the mountains, where the sun dreamed slow in summer.

Before, there was a boy called Koos, who lived in the city and was lonely and sad. His life was bad and his mother did not love him enough. So he was taken away from that place and brought to the village in the valley where he would be safe. And he *was* safe from the dangers that threatened him in the city. But in his heart was a cold, cold place where he was afraid. Koos looked at other boys, who had families and love and laughter on sunny mornings, and he hated them.

This story is about these people.

1

It was raining when Mubi came. Not raining hard so that he was really wet, as he stood on the step with his hat in his hand, but a cool, soft rain, drifting like smoke on the afternoon, leaving silver drops caught in his grey hair.

'I have come,' Mubi said, 'to bring the child.'

The child then. When I looked past Mubi he was there, head down, looking at his bare, brown feet, or the worn mat on the step, or the dampened dust of the farmyard, I could not tell which.

I shook my head, impatient with the man and his demands. He asked something of me which I did not want to give.

'Baba, I have said. There can be no child.'

He twisted his hat between tired hands.

'But there is no one else.'

It was true. There was no one else. I wanted to close the door, hard shut, so that I could not see the face which did not plead. I wanted the old man and his grandson to go away, and more than away, to never have been, so that I would not be left with this feeling of guilt. It made me angry, the guilt, for I had done nothing. I had done nothing. And maybe that was where the problem lay. I shook my head.

'Baba . . .' The silence hung between us like something that was real. Almost I could touch it. The boy, Mponyane, was looking at me for the first time and

I saw in his eyes the conflict that must be in his mind. He reached out very gently and touched my arm. I could not take him. I could not do it. 'Baba,' I said firmly. 'Baba . . . I . . . will take the child.'

And that was how Mponyane came to live with us. And how could our lives ever have been the way they are, if he had not come?

Mponyane was looking at the worn bit of carpet on the step. Dull patterns coiled across its dusty surface and there was a knotted fringe, tangled beyond recovery. His feet, white from the dust of the road, stood neatly beside it, and the woman's feet in their shiny shoes, owning the step.

The child shivered a little. He wasn't cold. He was afraid. This place was strange and worrying and not like home. There were dogs and Mponyane didn't like dogs. They had strong snapping teeth and could bite and they ran as fast as the wind when a small boy was least expecting them, making no sound that Mponyane could hear. He eyed them warily but they were safely penned on the other side of a rusting fence made of chicken wire.

There was also a boy. Baba had given him this knowledge. Where was the boy? Mponyane desperately wanted to see the boy who was to be his *umtalaan*, his closest person. When he saw him he would know if this white boy would be his friend. This was important because Mponyane knew that, if he stayed, he must look after this boy and care for him always. This was to be his work. Baba had shown him this and Mponyane was proud that he was to have so great a responsibility.

The woman was speaking, Mponyane knew this was so because her lips were moving, the pink cave of her mouth opened and closed showing teeth white in her tired smile. She did not want Mponyane, he

4

knew that. She had already refused once to have him, that other time when Baba had brought him, when summer had lain over the valley like a hot hand and the dust had snarled at their feet. No, she had said, and Baba had put on his old hat with the oily place where his hands had held it for so many years, and they had gone home. This time, Mponyane knew, Baba did not intend to accept no for an answer.

It was a long way from their *kraal* in the mountains to this place. It was a fearful thing to think of the hours of walking that lay now between himself and his home. They had begun when the light from the stars washed clear and clean over the land and the long shadows of the *mealies* blurred into the dark of the ground. Baba had tied the laces of his shoes together and hung them round his neck. Mponyane had no shoes. Baba had taken an empty meal bag with some food for the journey. Mponyane had carried a sack with his few belongings inside. It lay lightly over his shoulder, banging against his back when he walked.

One foot and then the other, until the distance shrank before them. The small track from their place joined to the dirt road and then the dirt road joined to the big road and the tar, hard underfoot. They rested for a while, but Baba would not stop for long. One foot after the other, on the dry grass at the side of the road, in the dust and on the hard grey. One foot after the other, until Mponyane found that he could not remember his home and searched in panic through the places of his mind to find the pictures of the small brown hut where he lived with Baba, and the *mealie* patch growing at the side. One foot after the other, until they saw the black heaps that came from the coal mines. Baba was speaking now, to the woman. His lips moved steadily, calmly. He

5

would not be hurried. Mponyane looked shyly at her to see what could be read from her expression.

He liked her face. She was not-young, not-old and her eyes had small cracks where she had smiled often. But there was a sadness there too, and she was tired. Mponyane thought about what he knew. This woman had been part of the story of his family, and her name was known. She was in his mind already, just as his grandfather was and his mother had been. She was Baba's friend and she listened to him which was a thing the white people did not often do. She had come to their *kraal* in the years before, when Baba was not yet old, and she had learned to know their ways, and that was a thing the white people never did. Truly this was a person who was different, and her name would be remembered.

She was shaking her head. Did that mean that he would not stay? Like a small candle flame, hope began to glow in Mponyane. He would not have to watch as Baba walked away alone. He would go too, back to his own place. And then Mponyane remembered why they had come, and the small candle flame died again, and his heart was black. He must stay because Baba was old and alone and there was no one left who could care for a child. He must stay because there were things he must learn which were important, more important than running in the mountain grass when the frost was thick and white on it. More important than the happiness in his heart at his own place. She had stopped smiling now and her face was sad. Shyly Mponyane put out his hand and touched her sleeve. It was a touch light as the wing of a night moth, but she felt it and looked down at him with that sad-kind smile that she had given him before.

There was a time of nothing. The two big people

were still. And then she put her hand on Mponyane's head and he knew that she had decided. Baba was smiling now, so Mponyane understood that her decision was what the old man wanted. She was smiling at him and at Baba, and their smiles joined so that even though he was afraid, Mponyane smiled a little too. He thought in his mind what she would be saying. Welcome, she would tell him, and be happy, she would say. But Mponyane could not hear her words. There was no hearing in his ears, and no words in his mouth. Since he had been born, Mponyane had been deaf and he could not speak.

2

Mponyane had known for a long time that he was different from the others. There was something they could do that he couldn't. It was the mouth movements. They all did them, but Mponyane didn't know what they meant. Baba had taught him one once, and that had taken such a long time that Baba had never tried to teach him any more. The two of them had sat in the sun every day for a week and Baba had made a mouth shape and pointed to himself. Over and over and over he had done it, until, just to please him, Mponyane had done the same thing. The old man had laughed and clapped his hands, so Mponyane did it again. Baba had liften Mponyane's hand to his lips so that his grandson could feel the shape that they made, feel the way that they changed when he made the mouth movements.

'Ba-Ba. Ba-ba. Ba-ba. Ba-ba. Ba-ba.' Until Mponyane was tired of the game and wished they could stop.

'Ba-ba. Ba-ba. Ba-ba.' Mponyane tried. He thought he was doing the right thing, but there must still have been something wrong.

'Ba-ba. Ba-ba.' The sun was hot and Mponyane was thirsty. He wanted a drink of cool water. He wanted to play with his clay oxen that Baba had made for him. And he didn't understand what was wrong.

At last Mubi had let the boy go. He watched Mponyane as he ran to the hut and his eyes were sad. Mponyane was making the right shapes with his mouth, but there was no sound. No sound at all.

Inside his head, where his other life was, Mponyane called the woman by a thought shape, which was Kra. There was no special reason for choosing this shape, except that he liked it. It was strong and kind, like a smile shape, and the woman had smiled at him as if she knew him, so she would be Kra when he thought of her. His outside world might be still and silent and quiet, but in his mind there were shapes for things that only he knew how to use.

Kra stood with him and watched as Mubi became a smaller and smaller figure on the road away, and eventually disappeared altogether. Mponyane's eyes prickled with the effort of seeing, as the old man dwindled out of his life.

She put her hand on his shoulder and the pressure of it was warm. Almost, Mponyane thought, as if she knew what he was feeling, although he did not know how she could. For another moment they stood like that, fixed, immobile in the light drift of rain until Mponyane could sense her small impatience travelling from her, through his shoulder to his arm, but she did not hurry him. Mponyane felt as though his feet were stuck down to the piece of carpet. He didn't want to move, as though staying where he was would stop things from happening to him. On the other side of the door was a new world which he did not know, and did not want to know.

But at last she turned to go, indicating that Mponyane should go with her and there was no longer any escape. Dutifully Mponyane picked up his sack and followed her inside.

The place was full of things. Things that glittered and shone and were white, or red, or yellow. There

9

was a table with vegetables on it ready for peeling, a chair with a bright cushion, a red rug on the floor, shelves with blue plates. So many objects that his eyes did not know where to look, so Mponyane closed them for a moment instead, and saw the familiar belongings of his old life.

In his own place, when he had stepped through the door of their hut, there had been a pattern that never varied, and the shapes were as familiar to him as the lines on the palm of his hand. Briefly he felt that he was there again and there sprang into the place, behind his seeing, a picture of the brown walls of Baba's hut, the brown floor of Baba's hut, and the smooth black polished pots that rested on the brown. The blanket that covered the old iron bed was blue striped with green, and washed so often that the colours had softened and smudged into each other. There was a shelf where Baba's things were kept, the tin cups and the tobacco jar and the candlestick. And there was the cardboard box where Mponyane kept his winter jersey and his other pair of shorts.

But a picture of his place was not the real place. Sadly Mponyane opened his eyes again, and there was the boy, standing shyly, looking at him sideways as if *he* was the one who was new and frightened.

The boy was about six years old, much smaller than Mponyane and sturdier, with fair hair and blue eyes, the way Mponyane had imagined he would be; like the pictures in the old book Baba sometimes looked at, the one the wife of Mr Van Niekerk had been throwing away when Baba went to the farm to take wood. But Mponyane realized that this boy was not like the children in the book, who played and laughed in a green place where the sun always shone. This boy was sad and afraid. Mponyane could sense, beating inside him, the black bruise on his heart where the hurt was.

He did not know what he should do, and the waiting time stretched on and on and became uncomfortable.

Then, slowly, the boy held out his hand. Mponyane gripped his sack tighter. He did not know white people, except for Mr Van Niekerk who came sometimes to the end of the hard road in his truck when he wanted men to come and work for him. Mr Van Niekerk was old, with a red face and white hair, and Mponyane had never been close enough to him to find out exactly how he was different from black people, so what could that help?

The boy put down his outstretched hand and there was a look on his face now as if he did not know what to do next. Then he touched Mponyane's arm lightly, and made some mouth shapes. Mponyane looked very hard at the mouth shapes, but still didn't know what they meant.

Kra had been watching them quietly, but now she started making shapes again. She put her hand on the boy's head.

'Frank,' she said, slowly and carefully. 'F-r-a-n-k.'

Inside his head Mponyane thought a name picture that might mean the same as the shape.

'Fan,' that was what he would call the boy.

Mponyane put his head on one said and studied Fan again. He wore blue shorts, not new, and a paler blue shirt. There were brown sandals on his feet with shiny buckles.

Fan was smiling a little now, but it was not a strong smile, as if it might go away unless something happened soon. Mponyane thought that perhaps he must be the one to act first, because he was older. He took the sack from his shoulder and fumbled inside it until he found the toy oxen. The clay was smooth under Mponyane's reluctant fingers. Baba

11

had made these. But he held them out to Fan and Fan's eyes widened.

'Look Mom!' he said to his mother. 'Clay oxen! I haven't had any since Dad. . .' He paused for a moment. 'Since Dad went away.'

The clay oxen lay heavy in Frank's hand. But there wasn't very much else in the sack, Frank could see that. Maybe this boy didn't have many toys. On a sudden impulse he handed back one of the oxen. They would play with them together anyway. When he saw the expression in Mponyane's eyes he was glad that he had thought of that.

Kra's words:

That first day when Mponyane came to live with us, I was angry with myself. What had I done? Taken responsibility for a boy who could neither hear nor speak, who would have to be fed – and there was little enough money for the three of us as it was – who would have to be cared for and comforted when he was sad, punished when he was naughty; another burden. I stood in my kitchen after the boys had gone out to the yard, and everywhere I looked there were problems so huge and so threatening that I felt I could never overcome them. I had just accepted the problem of a silent child who could not hear. And why? And why?

It had started, I suppose, with Maina. My friend Maina. Thin she was, with the kind of whippy strength that never falters. Young she had been then too, although that had soon gone, and her satin brown skin had glowed with health. Mubi brought her to the small mine house we had in those days and pushed her gently forward.

'She is my son's wife,' he said, and Maina smiled her shy and secret smile with eyes cast down. 'She will help you with your daughter and the small one.'

In the background, as if knowing that he was the subject of discussion, the small one yelled his usual determined wail and I felt a sudden crushing weariness and the realization that I did not have the strength to go to him.

I must have nearly fainted, I think, for when I next knew what was around me, I was sitting at my own kitchen table, staring at the patterns in the grain of the wood and trying to remember what it was that had been so urgent in my mind. There was something different. What was missing? And then I realized that, for almost the first time in three months I was awake and the baby wasn't crying.

It was like coming home after that.

I don't think Frank would have survived without Maina. He was so sick, poor child. My husband Etienne often had to be away and I was unutterably weary. I think the baby would have slipped from me as my thoughts had just slipped from my mind. One night I would have fallen asleep, because I could not stay awake, and when I woke there would have been no more crying.

Maina saved Frank and I think she saved me as well. Etienne travelled a lot in those days, going to different mines, learning how other systems worked, planning the new way that would come for the future. He worried about us a lot. I know that. His eyes, as he came through the door were always anxious, until Maina came, fearing what I might tell him. Frank was so sick; so sick. But with Maina there I felt safe. She had a son, I knew that, back at her kraal. She told me he was six years old, but she never told me he was unable to hear or speak. Not then. That I only found out when it was time for her to go back, when she was ill herself and needed to be with her own people again, and in her own place.

Maina was like Frank's other mother. He was ill

for months. His arms and legs were so skinny and weak, and his skin so transparent that at times we despaired of saving him. He lay so still in his cot that we would often lean over anxiously to feel whether he still breathed. Maina was always there, always ready to nurse him for a while so that I could rest, or to tie him onto her back while she worked about the house so that I could fetch Cecily from her play-school. I paid her a wage at the end of each week, but Maina was more than an employee. She was my friend.

I remember feeling ashamed, that day when Mponyane came, that I had ever thought of not accepting Maina's child. It would have been easier to have said no to Mubi. It would have been easier to have pretended that Mponyane did not exist. That he was not deaf. That he did not need my help. It would have been easier, but I could not take that way.

3

Frank led the way out of the kitchen, and Mponyane followed. Kra had taken his sack, but each boy still held one of Mubi's clay oxen. The rain had stopped and a thin sun tried to warm the damp ground.

Frank looked doubtfully at Mponyane. He wasn't used to having company, except sometimes his sister Cecily, and she didn't count because she was a girl and also too old to be interesting. There were no other young people on their farm, no children. Everyone had gone away to the cities except old Induna, who was too tired to go, and a few women who were waiting for their men to send for them. Frank supposed he ought to suggest some kind of entertainment.

'Let's go and play at the dam,' he said. Mponyane said nothing. Frank was not sure what to do next. He knew Mponyane couldn't hear him, but it felt wrong not to speak. Rude almost. Maybe if he shouted?

'The dam!' he yelled. 'Let's play at the dam!'

Mponyane smiled faintly, but still said nothing. Frank looked at him anxiously. Did it hurt, he wondered, to be deaf?

They would probably have stood there longer if it had not been for the yellow butterfly. It danced towards them in a shaft of light and its wings caught and held the flash of gold. Both boys turned to watch. Hesistantly Mponyane put down his clay ox. What was he going to do? Frank laid his down as well. Mponyane was looking at him with a gleam of mischief in his eyes. He raised his arms at his sides. Frank copied him. For a moment they stood like that and then Mponyane was off, whirling his arms and flapping them in a wild parody of the graceful butterfly and Frank was after him, running and whooping and laughing. They ended up at the dam anyway.

After that Frank just talked when he felt like talking. He felt more comfortable that way, and Mponyane didn't mind.

Maybe words were not important to Mponyane, Frank thought, because he had another world, a world of his own that was different and fascinating and not scary. Mponyane saw things and felt things that Frank had never noticed before. He saw the way that the birds flew low against the hill in the evening and he saw the silver drops caught in the early morning leaves, and he showed these things to Frank, with signs. He could talk, in a way, without sounds.

The first time he did this, his hands made a spider crawling, crawling on a delicate web, then the spider was more real than a sound would have been. When Frank looked down at the living spider at his feet, he saw that its legs were at exactly the same angle as Mponyane's fingers, and it moved with just the same jerky grace as the boy had shown.

Frank looked round for something that he could show to Mponyane. This was a good game. There was a tree with a broken branch that had blown loose in the last big storm. Frank studied it carefully for a moment and then, with some difficulty, arranged his arm and hand, into the shape of the branch. Mponyane jumped up and down with delight, running to the tree and touching the branch, turning to grin at Frank. They played that game for some time before they came to a satisfying patch of mud beside the dam and settled down to make things.

It was good being with Mponyane, Frank thought. And safe, almost like when he and Dad used to come down here and Dad used to pretend he was fishing when he was really asleep. Shyly Frank looked over to where Mponyane was constructing a mud fort.

'Dad and I used to come here.'

Mponyane didn't react.

'I miss Dad.'

Mponyane slapped some more earth on the side wall.

'He's . . . he's in prison now.'

Mponyane looked up then, and saw Frank staring at him. He smiled.

Frank was relieved. 'Well, that's all right then. If you don't mind like the others.' He went over to help with the fort. It didn't occur to him that Mponyane hadn't heard a word he'd said. It was easy to forget that he was deaf.

Frank had also forgotten about the big boys from the school hostel. That didn't often happen. They hung at the back of his mind for most of the time – even when he was asleep. Often he was more afraid of them when they weren't there, than when they were. When they were actually twisting his arm behind his back, or throwing lighted matches down his shirt, he at least knew what the worst was going to be. Or hoped he did. Before they came he had to wonder, and fear, what they would do.

This time it was an extra shock when the long shadow fell across the mud and a pair of dirty feet in flip-flops settled themselves in front of him. Frank didn't look up. He knew whose feet they were.

'Found yourself a friend, hey, Frankie-baby?'

'Ja,' the reply was almost a whisper.

'Found yourself a *black* friend, Frankie-baby?'

Frank looked up then. 'Ja. What's it to you, Koos?'

'What's it to me, Frankie? I'll tell you what it is to me, my man. As long as I'm around you have no friends. Not even,' the bigger boy turned to sneer at Mponyane, 'not even black rubbish friends.'

For the first time ever in his dealings with Kosie, Frank felt anger instead of fear.

'He's *not* rubbish and he *is* my friend!'

'Oh yes? And he knows all about little Frankie-baby, and all about little Frankie-baby's father, does he?' Not hurrying, Kosie turned to survey Mponyane who looked back at him without showing any particular emotion. 'Hey black rubbish, you want to be careful who you play with, boy. Even for you, this is low man, real low.'

Mponyane didn't say anything.

'Lost your tongue boy? Or just showing the proper respect for old Koos, eh?' Kosie laughed, and the sound was not a happy one. 'This – black rubbish – is white rubbish.' He kicked Frank thoughtfully, not hard. 'This kid has a father, man, who's the worst, man, the real worst. He's so bad that I have to make real sure his little boy don't grow up to follow in his footsteps. Ja, man, that's my job in life. Making sure old Frankie-baby don't turn out a bad lot like his Pa – or maybe even making sure that Frankie-baby don't turn out at all. Like, you know, maybe one dark night . . .' Kosie drew his finger across his throat and rolled his eyes expressively. 'Ja, man.'

Dully Frank looked down at the mud. Rising from beneath the black ooze were bubbles; three, four, five of them that popped gently when they reached the surface. What lived under there, where it was dark and cool, silent and safe? He wished he could crawl down and let the soft slime close over his head,

sealing him off from Kosie and the other boys for-
ever. Sealing him off and protecting him from Kosie's
voice that went on and on.

'The problem always is,' Kosie paused to give his
words more effect. 'The problem always is, just how
to teach little Frankie.'

Inside himself Frank felt the little wobble of fear.
This was when he usually got hurt. A long arm
reached down and a bony hand grabbed his elbow.

'Like maybe the old arm twisting isn't as sore as it
used to be . . .' Kosie gave Frank's arm a vicious twist
just to make sure. 'Or maybe we ought to . . .' But
Frank didn't hear what new torment Kosie had
devised for that day. There was a sudden crack, a
howl of pain from Kosie, and Frank felt himself dropped as suddenly as he had been caught up. Kosie
was standing back holding his fingers against his
chest, an expression of pained amazement on his
face. Mponyane was standing in front of him holding
a long whippy stick he had picked up.

There was a moment of confrontation when it was
uncertain what would happen next, and then Kosie
turned on his heel and left. He didn't go far though,
before he turned to call back to Frank.

'Don't think I'm going to forget this, Frankie-baby.
Oh, no. I'm not going to forget this. Ever.' And then
he was gone.

Shakily Frank got to his feet. Mponyane stroked
his arm softly, looking the question.

'It's all right,' Frank said. Then he remembered.
He nodded and smiled and rubbed his arm to show
that it didn't hurt – and it didn't. Well, not as much
as it usually did, because this time he had a friend
who had helped him and would help him again.
How could he thank Mponyane? Words were no
good. What was left? Touch, he supposed. Awkwardly

Frank put his good arm round the other boy's shoulders.

'Friend,' he said slowly, making the shape of the word clearly with his mouth. 'My friend.' And Mponyane, anxious to show that he understood, made the same mouth movement.

'Friend,' he mouthed, just as Frank had done. 'Friend.'

It didn't matter that there was no sound. They understood one another.

But inside Mponyane's head as he followed Frank home, were many new things.

4

There was a girl when they came home. Mponyane
had expected her. Mubi had shown him with signs
that there would be one. She was tall and fair and
her hair was long and shining like sunshine and her
smile was like her mother's smile.

She nodded a welcome to Mponyane and then
turned to her brother, 'Frankie, have those hostel
boys been at you again?' There were still faint tracks
in the dirt on Frank's face where a tear or two had
run through.

'Nah,' he said shortly. 'Not much. Just Koos. Mponyane hit him with a stick. He's my friend.'

She turned to look again at the small Zulu boy.
He was about her age, she supposed, about twelve,
but small and wiry looking. He'd have to be tough
if he wanted to take on Kosie and his lot. Maybe he
had to be extra tough anyway. It couldn't be easy to
be deaf.

Cecily knew about Kosie and his gang because they
were in her class. They'd tried it with her as well,
after the court case. It had felt as if everyone in the
world was against them then, and the only people
who *would* speak to them were saying things they
didn't want to hear. Cecily hadn't cared much, not
then. She was hurting too much from the real things,
from Dad going and from the accident to let them
bully her with words, and they hadn't dared touch

her, not with Mr Kruger in the hostel and the things he had to say about boys who roughed the girls up.

He was fair, was Mr Kruger, and he didn't hesitate to lay about him with his stick when the boys got out of hand. Especially those who were in the hostel as a place-of-safety-from-something-worse in Durban. Sometimes Cecily wondered what could be worse than having to live in the hostel with Mr Kruger, but her imagination failed her every time.

Mr Ross, the Principal, had spoken to the whole school at assembly the day before Kosie had arrived. He had used words like 'disadvantaged' and 'welfare' and 'unsuitable', but the children had understood what he was telling them.

A boy was coming who was unhappy and they must be kind to him. Maybe they would have been, but then there was the accident and there was no room left in their minds for caring about someone they didn't know. Maybe, Cecily thought, *she* should have. She knew he watched her when he thought she wasn't looking. Perhaps it would be a good thing to think outside her own pain and reach out to someone else's.

Mponyane reached out and touched the girl's arm. Why was she so sad? What had changed her face and taken away her smile? His touch brought Cecily back, and her smile too.

'I'm Cecily,' she said clearly and slowly. 'Cec-il-y.'

Mponyane mouthed the shape back at her. 'Cecy-cy.'

'No, Cec-il-y.'

'Cecy-cy.'

Cecily smiled and shrugged. She would just have to be Cecy. And that was close enough to the Zulu word for sister. 'Come on you boys. Wash up. You're covered in mud.'

Which, Frank thought, was typical of sisters. He

had never told Cecily all that happened when Kosie and his gang got hold of him. He didn't want her to worry. She worried a lot as it was.

Mponyane felt a small warmth in his heart. These people would be kind to him. He had a place, and an important job to do, which was to look after his umtalaan, his special person, Fan. He had Kra to look after as well and this sister-person who was called a shape which meant Cecy. Life would be kind to him here.

If it wasn't for the dogs! They came bounding in right then, three of them, and Frank laughed to see the expression of horror on Mponyane's face.

'Haai! They won't hurt you!'

The dogs tumbled and leapt and licked at Fan's face. There were three of them, brown and gold dotted with white patches. Pink tongues waved like flags and short stumpy legs darted them busily about.

'This is Ting-a-ling. We call him that because he has a bell on his collar. And this is Pannekoek because he has a pancake shape over one eye – and this,' Fan bent down to pick up the largest of the three dogs and stroked its head, 'is my very special dog Boelie.'

This meant nothing to Mponyane, but he could see that the dogs, and especially the last one Fan had held up against him, were his umtalaan's friends. Mponyane sighed. There had to be something wrong of course. Reluctantly he held out a hand. He knew they would bite him, but it was his duty to make friends with the animals of Fan. He closed his eyes and retreated into the dark and silent world that was his when he could not see. He waited for the pain.

There was none. Just soft licking feelings where the dogs were making friends with him. Cautiously Mponyane opened his eyes and there was Fan laughing and the dogs jumping and opening and closing their big pink mouths in a friendly way. The warm place inside Mponyane became larger, and the happiness grew. It would be all right.

Kra's words:

After that day it was as though Mponyane had always been with us. In the mornings I would call Frank and Cecily and wake him with a little shake and he always awoke smiling. It was a good thing to begin the day with: Mponyane smiling. He had a smile of such sweetness, as though it could say for him all the things he could not speak himself. The Zulus believe that a child like Mponyane is a special child, a life-gift and should be treasured as such. After I knew Mponyane, I was sure that this was so. He was not able to hear, but he felt things so much more.

Sometimes I grieved for him. When he was older he would be hurt – I was sure of this, and maybe he sensed it too. It was as though, in those last days of his childhood, he was determined to enjoy every moment that he could.

He made a difference to Frank. Before he came Frank had been withdrawn and quiet. A heaviness rested on him. I had thought he was too young to understand the court case and all it implied. Maybe I had been wrong. But with Mponyane he was another boy. The two of them – and the dogs – ranged far and wide over the farm, and played, and got incredibly dirty, and behaved just like normal children would. For a time I forgot about the village and the hate.

Mponyane had only one sound. It was a kind of a laugh, although sometimes it could be a cry of despair and sometimes it was a murmur of sympathy.

'He-he-he-he-he HEY!' he would shout when he was happy.

'Hey-hey, Hey-hey!' he would cry in alarm.

'Heya, Heya,' he would say softly when he was sad for me, and sometimes he would touch my cheek gently with the backs of his fingers to show that he cared.

Frank was seven that year. He should have been at school already, but the long illness when he was a baby had left him weak and delicate and Dr de Wit had said he must wait a year. I was not sorry. It gave him time to run free for a while before he had to settle into a routine and the time strengthened him. After Mponyane came he began to go out more, and stuck less closely to me. Mponyane was young, but I trusted him implicitly after a few days. He would, I knew, look after my son. He proved it to me within a week.

'Haai, Mponyane!' Frank still forgot sometimes. Mponyane was looking the other way, watching the chickens fighting over some bread crusts, and could not understand. Frank shook his head and went over to touch Mponyane on the shoulder. Mponyane swung round at once.

'Dam,' Frank mouthed. He was trying to teach Mponyane some words by making shapes, but it was hard work. Frank supposed it must be a lot more difficult than it looked. But 'dam' was fairly easy, especially as they always went there afterwards and he used the word often while they were there. He had given up with the dogs' names. Ting-a-ling and Pannekoek and Boelie seemed to be too complicated to teach to a deaf person. They used signs instead.

Mponyane nodded eagerly. He knew this shape. He had a dream about learning all the hundreds of mouthshapes that the others made. Then he would be able to give out ideas quickly, like they did, instead of having to make signs and act out what he wanted to share. The inside of his head sometimes felt like a cageful of butterflies that were trying to get out. The wings of ideas beat and beat against the side of his skull, but could not escape.

He nodded again, making the word shape for the water place, and Fan was pleased. They collected the dogs and ran, pretending to be red-legged locusts, jumping and zigzagging crazily with their elbows stuck out.

'He-he-HEY!' Mponyane shouted.

'Wow-eeeee!' Frank screamed. And the wind of their running was freedom.

The dam was their special, favourite place. The summer rains were late, only a few isolated showers had fallen. Not enough. The cracked mud crept inwards toward the depth of the water, and in the dry reed beds were secret things and silent places. Frank led the way, as he always did, and they crept like careful hunters through the crackle-dry stems until they reached their hiding place. Mponyane pulled a pile of reeds behind them and they were invisible, as if they had never been.

They dared not light a fire because of the drought, although Frank would dearly have liked to roast sweet potatoes and eat them steaming hot from the flames as he had once done when . . . well, as he had once done; with Dad. Before the court case had come and messed everything up. They had been friends, him and Dad.

Instead of sweet potatoes they had some cooked *mealies* left over from supper last night and Mponyane had some chocolate which Kra had given him and which he had forgotten in his pocket. It was a feast. Afterwards they settled back, contemplating the peace which for Frank meant the absence of Kosie and his mob, the silence of the quiet water.

Mponyane always had quiet. It was something he carried with him. But the peace of the late afternoon and the lack of activity was restful. Sometimes he got awfully tired of trying to understand. Times like this were rare, when nobody was trying to tell him anything, and there were no mouth movements to watch hopelessly.

Mponyane felt himself drifting on the edge of sleep. His mind played idly over the events of the day – breakfast of putu porridge. Fan and he had made a little man out of the stiff porridge and had taken turns to bite off the legs and arms, although Mponyane had, of course, insisted that Fan ate the head. They had built a *kraal* out of stones up at the barn and defended it against each other. Mponyane had allowed Fan to win. And there had been corned beef for lunch which was one of the few things of their food that Mponyane liked. A good day.

And then came the small prickle of warning that Mponyane had felt before. Only twice had he felt it, the time when his mother had been sick and he had run back to the hut too late to say goodbye, and the time when Baba had broken his leg and Mponyane had been the only one who could guess, or sense, where he was.

Abruptly Mponyane sat up. The sun had slipped a little further down while his eyes had been closed. There was a chill little wind and soon it would be dark. Mponyane felt angry with himself. He had not been guarding his umtalaan as he should – and there *was* danger. He was certain of it now.

There was an icy feeling along the back of his neck – fear and a little guilt mixed with something else. Anger maybe? When he found the danger, what could he do? There was nobody to help and he could not bring people with the mouth shapes as the others could. Mponyane felt again the bitterness of his anger. Why was *he* different?

And then he saw the snake.

This was the worst thing that could happen. For Mponyane was truly afraid of snakes. He had not been afraid when that big white boy with the red hair and blotchy face had tried to hurt Fan. He had not been afraid – well not much – when the dogs had been sure to bite him. He would not, he knew, be afraid when a bull charged, or a lion even. But he was afraid of snakes.

It was a green snake and Mponyane knew that they were the worst kind. Death came soon when a green snake struck – and it was creeping slowly towards Fan who dreamed still of whatever mind shapes he knew. Fan's eyes were closed and he was smiling.

Mponyane moved carefully, but not carefully enough. The snake saw him move. Its horrible little black eyes slid like dark oil over Fan. Its tongue flickered so fast that the movement was a blur. It raised itself on its coils and drew back its head. Desperately Mponyane flung himself across Fan and grabbed the snake. He had it by the throat, but it could still twist round towards his hand – and did so. Mponyane crawled to his feet, staggered over the struggling Fan and whirled the snake above his head, smashing it again and again against the trunk of a wattle tree until he was certain it must be dead.

They took the snake with them. Home to Kra. Frank was excited. For him it had been an adventure. Mponyane was silent. For him it had been terrible. Not the snake. He realized now that he was not really afraid of snakes – well, not as much as he had thought. But Fan had been so close to that evil and Fan was his special person. Baba had given him this

responsibility. Baba had trusted his grandson and
Mponyane had nearly failed – as he had failed in
everything else he had tried to do. A picture came
to Mponyane's mind of the other boys going off to
the veld with their hunting sticks. Baba had held him
back with one hand on his arm. He had smiled, but
his smile had been sad. Mponyane had known then
that he would never be like the others. Always he
would be different and always Baba would be sad
because of that.

Kra's words:

I can never forget the night of the snake. They
came, the two of them, in procession from the direction of the dam. I had already been anxious. It was
late, almost dark and I began to think of all the
things that could have happened. The unreasonable
fears that only a mother would imagine.

As they came under the light of the electric bulb
on the stoep I saw at once that Frank was unharmed.
He was flushed and agitated, but all right. Mponyane
was a different matter. He was drained; grey with
fear or dread, I could not tell which. Without any
expression in his eyes he held up the mamba for me
to see. It was all of four feet long.

I don't think I even screamed, I was so shocked.
And then I realized how seriously Mponyane was
affected. He was almost rigid. His jaw seemed to be
wired together and sweat stood out all over him. I
showed him that he must put down the snake, but
he didn't seem able to let it go. By now I was really
concerned. I managed to pull myself together and
tried to take the dead snake from him. His fingers
were clenched so tightly around it that I could not
loosen them. I took his head between both of my
hands and shook him gently.

'Mponyane! You must put down the snake!'

Slowly his eyes focused on mine and gradually he loosened his grip. Behind me Frank was very quiet. I sank down beside Mponyane, still looking into his eyes. How could we communicate? How could I comfort him? Frank came up beside me and I put my arms round both boys, holding them close, holding them tight. Mponyane didn't cry, but slowly I felt the tension go out of him until he rested limply against me. Then I took them into the house and gave them hot milk and sugar and put them to bed.

But I could not settle after they slept. It was the first time I really saw what it must be like; to be deaf and not to be able to hear words of comfort and to be made dumb by deafness and be unable to speak your trouble.

At midnight Mponyane came from his room and he showed me with signs that he wanted to know where I had put the snake. Together, by torch-light, we buried it deep in the flowerbed beside the dried up fountain. Buried it deep, so that the nightmares would go too.

In the morning there were flowers on the grave.

5

It was quiet on the farm. There was a rhythm to the days that brought a certain comfort. Early in the morning old Induna would bang an iron pipe against a bit of railway track that hung from the pepper tree, and a chattering flock of Zulu women would descend on the farmyard, smiling and laughing with each other. Induna would solemnly allocate their tasks for the day. Two to hoe the cabbage field where the small green seedlings were just pushing through the dry ground. Two to clean the chicken house and collect the eggs. One to chase the herd of thin cattle onto the veld and watch them while they grazed. Induna himself did no real work. He was too old. Instead he dozed beside the hut where the tools were kept and maintained a dignified appearance for any visitors who might come.

Not that there were many of those. The extension officer came once or twice a year to advise Kra. Usually he just shook his head instead of making any suggestions. There was little point in recommending a new fertilizer where there was no money to buy any. The Government vet trundled up the road when he was in the neighbourhood, raising a cloud of dust behind his ancient red bakkie.[1] One momentous

[1.] truck

afternoon the bank manager arrived in his Mercedes. He didn't stay long.

There was only one other visitor, and she travelled out from the village because she wanted to, rather than had to in the line of business. Lisa Ross, the new headmaster's wife, came once and had tea and stale biscuits, but she and Kra didn't seem to have much to talk about. They sat rather awkwardly in the lounge that was hardly ever used and, although Kra sensed that this woman was friendly and might even *be* a friend one day, she was embarrassed by her own obvious poverty and unsure whether Lisa Ross had heard their story. Part of her wanted to be dignified and aloof in case Lisa was unaware of their circumstances, and the other part wanted to break down and just talk to another woman. It was difficult to be natural in the circumstances and neither of them was satisfied with the encounter when Lisa eventually left.

Every evening when Induna had collected the hoes and the spades (counting them carefully as if they might mysteriously have dwindled in number, and stacking them in the tool-hut before he padlocked them in) a silence fell over the farm that was unbroken by music or laughter or any kind of life. Kra would be bone tired – she worked much harder than anyone else on the farm, ploughing great clouds of dust about with the rickety tractor when it was that time of the year and then dragging the water tank behind it when the green spikes broke the surface. If it was term time, Cecily would have homework. Frank and Mponyane went to bed early, as soon as their supper was finished and Mponyane had washed the dishes.

The routine was very seldom broken, so it was a surprise to all of them one Sunday afternoon when a smart green car pulled up in the farmyard, and an elderly man with a big white moustache got out. The house was in a mess. Kra had not had any energy left to tidy up after lunch and the boys were making wire cars all over the kitchen floor. Mponyane could see that Kra was caught at a disadvantage. She fluttered and flustered around trying to straighten the cushions and clear away the plates.

The old man seemed to be irritated by all this activity. He nodded at Frank, allowed Cecily to kiss him on the cheek and shook Kra's hand. Maybe, Mponyane thought, he was the Baba of Fan. There was something in the two faces that showed they had the same blood.

For a while it did not go well. There was anger, Mponyane could see that, and the old man was redder in the face, waving his arms about. Kra was shaking her head. She had that proud look she wore when things were not right or when there was no money. Maybe the anger *was* about money, because at one point the old man took out his wallet and flourished a thick wad of ten rand notes, but Kra still shook her head.

And then suddenly the tension was gone and the old man was smiling, and shaking his own head, but ruefully as though Kra had somehow done what he expected her to do. He went out to the shiny green car, waving for Mponyane to follow him. Fan, of course, came too. There were boxes all over the back seat with food and some bottles as well. The old man made mouth shapes, but luckily also made more arm-wavings, so Mponyane knew that he must carry the boxes inside. Fan helped.

Kra sat down weakly at the kitchen table looking at the boxes and her eyes had water in them, something that Mponyane had not seen before. The Baba of Fan took one of the bottles of brown liquid and poured some for Kra and some for himself, and they sat for a long time making mouth movements. Every so often the Baba of Fan would help himself to some more of the stuff in the bottle and his face was redder still and he laughed a lot.

It was quite boring, so the two boys went back to their wire cars. The dogs lay on the floor beside them with their tongues hanging out and their breath coming in short blasts which meant that they were hot from running in the veld.

After a while Kra went to make some food with some of the things from the boxes, and the old man sat staring in front of him with his glass in his hand, looking sad. He had some more of the brown liquid and looked even more unhappy. Sometimes his eyes rested on Fan, busy with his cars, and he would drink again from the glass, until at last it slipped from his hand and rested on its side on the square of carpet, and he was asleep.

The wire cars were finished, and the boys had played with them enough. Fan was lying with his head on Boelie's back, kicking his feet against one of the chairs, and Mponyane didn't think this was a good thing for him to do while the old man was here. They had been to the dam already today and up onto the koppie with their brown-paper kites. Suddenly Fan sat up and there was a sparkle in his eyes that meant mischief.

'Come on, Mponyane!'

He jumped to his feet, showing Mponyane that he must be very quiet. Lying with the glass, beside the chair on the square of carpet, was a strange thing. Mponyane had never seen anything like it. It was the teeth of the old man! Mponyane's eyes were round as marbles. This was truly a wonderful thing, to take the teeth out of the head when he slept. His own

Baba still had many fine, white teeth, but he could not take them out for a rest like this.

At once the boys were a Zulu impi, with Fan in the lead, creeping through the dense bush on the lounge floor, awash with dangers, to their target – the teeth.

It wasn't their fault exactly, that Ting-a-ling chose to take an interest in their game. And they hadn't expected him to make a grab for the teeth while they were still in the middle of the dense carpet-bush. He just rushed up behind them, grabbed the teeth and was off out the front door before they could stop him.

'Hey-Hey-HEY!' Mponyane said softly. This was bad.

There were plenty of places Ting-a-ling could have chosen to hide the teeth. He decided on the coal shed. Hotly pursued by Boelie, Pannekoek – and a small Zulu impi – he rushed across the farmyard, through the hole in the door where the boards had come loose, scraped a neat hole in the coal to hide his new treasure in, and backed out of the hole again. Somehow it seemed to him like a good idea to go and hunt for dangerous beasts in the veld for a while.

It took some time to find the teeth again, even after Fan had found the key to the shed and his torch. Both boys got rather dirty while they were looking, so that by the time they emerged into daylight with the teeth triumphantly held aloft, they were covered in coal dust.

Mponyane looked at Fan and Fan looked at Mponyane. Fan grinned.

'Same colour Mponyane!' he said happily, holding his own black arm against Mponyane's. 'We're both black!'

But he was not really black enough, so he stripped

off his T-shirt and, with Mponyane's help, made a better job of it so that his smile was as white in his face as Mponyane's, and they both felt that now they would make a much more realistic impi.

And it was at precisely that moment that the roar of rage came from the direction of the house.

Kra's words:

It was good to see Etienne's father. We had our differences of course, as we always would, and he still thought that money was the answer to everything. But Etienne had never taken a cent from the old devil, and I knew he wouldn't want me to start now. We would manage.

It was strange hearing my husband's name said by someone else. Sometimes before I went to sleep, when the house was still and quiet and the children slept, I would say his name out loud. Just to hear it in the silence. It had been nearly a year now, a whole year, and I was sure there was nobody else who still believed in him. Even his own father had his doubts. But Etienne had told me he was innocent, and that was enough for me, even if all the courts and judges in the land disagreed with me.

Well, there were only another three years to wait and he would be back with us. Three years. Frank would be ten.

I thought the old man was having a heart attack when he shouted – bellowed – from the sitting-room. But when I got there he was dancing up and down too much for that to be the case. He also seemed to have lost his teeth.

'Those blasted kids had stolen my teeth!' he yelled, jumping up and down with rage and so red in the face that I thought he really might bring a coronary on.

'Blasted kids! Blasted kids!'

Cecily came running down from her room at the noise. I had to look away when she caught my eye. It really was too funny. But I did have my suspicions about Frank. It was just the kind of mischief he liked.

And I was right. The screen door from the stoep banged open and an apparition of coal dust stood there with Mponyane. Mponyane just looked dirty, Frank was black as soot. In one grimy hand he held out a grimy set of false teeth.

'We found these in the coal shed, Grandpa,' he said by way of explanation.

Etienne's father wasn't impressed.

6

Mponyane did not forget Kosie. There had been something in the tall white boy's face that reminded Mponyane of the green snake. Something cold and cruel that had nothing to do with the normal teasing of boys who are friends. Because he couldn't hear, Mponyane used his other senses to read the people around him. He looked and he really saw, where others might only listen. He had looked at Kosie and instead of the tough, street-wise fighter that most people found because they expected to, Mponyane sensed a damaged heart and mind that had left a black place in Kosie, a black place where bad things could grow. Who could have done this thing? Mponyane didn't know, but he was afraid for Fan.

There was not a lot that he could do to prepare Fan, to give him protection, but when he had been younger, Mponyane had learned with the other boys of his age, the skills of fighting with sticks. Now he began to teach these to Fan. It was a game of course, but one that they played every day until Fan was as good as Mponyane had been when he was seven years old.

'Haai, Mponyane! Haven't we done enough?'

But Mponyane would pick up the fighting sticks one more time and play the game again. They carried their sticks everywhere and the dogs were always with them.

Mponyane had grown used to the dogs now. In a way they shared something, those dogs and Mponyane, because they both had charge of Fan. And they all loved him. Fan had been so lonely before.

This was something that puzzled Mponyane. In his own village there was friendship. Even when times were hard – especially when times were hard – the people were together. Most of the men were away, working on the mines or on the farms, and the women helped each other. If food was short, they shared. If there was no money, somebody found that they had a little to spare. And they laughed together. When Kra took the boys on a rare trip into the village, nobody laughed with her.

Some of the men would tip their hats to her and look away, embarrassed and the storekeeper sometimes made a few mouth movements, but they were cold; cold and hard. There was nothing in Mponyane's experience which could explain why this was so. Again he felt that slow anger feeling which he had more often now. What had Kra done? What could be so bad that her own people cut her out of their lives? And why couldn't he, Mponyane, understand more?

There was so much which happened quickly, when people were turned away from him. There was so much that he couldn't see, so he couldn't know. Before, when his life had been simpler, he had managed to make up the things that he missed, to fill in the gaps on his own. Now the spaces in between the things that he understood were larger and larger, so that he could not stretch his mind far enough to bridge them. Mponyane sometimes felt very old, although he was only twelve, and the time when he had been young seemed to be a long way in the past.

Still the rains did not come and the land was dry

and dusty. It was a summer of butterflies that year. They were everywhere, in great golden-white clouds, touching the earth with dancing wings. The dam shrank under the onslaught of the sun, and the green things faded and dried. There was electricity in the air so that the dogs' fur sparked when they were stroked.

Mponyane and Fan ranged far and wide over the farm. For the first time Mponyane had someone who did not know more than he did. There were things that he could show Fan. Things about the veld and the animals that lived there. Things that his own people had always known. Because Fan was so young there were none of the puzzles Mponyane found with older people. It was a good time.

Once they crept out of Fan's window when it was newly dark. The dogs were pleased to see them, wagging their stumpy tails and licking the boys' hands. Mponyane felt very brave and important. He was going to show Fan night animals and teach him about night things. Kra was sitting in the kitchen with a book. She would not look in on them until she went to bed and that was hours away. Cecy was asleep. Nobody would ever know they had been out.

The farm was different at night. A very slim moon lit their way. Mponyane was in the lead, Fan behind, and the dogs followed. They were heading for the field where the pumpkins grew and Mponyane hoped there would be porcupines. The night was heady with the sweet smell of wattle flowers and dust. Mponyane waved his stick and grinned back at Fan.

Once they were well clear of the house they began to run along the smooth beaten path, their feet pounding together on the hard ground. Running like an impi, Mponyane thought, like real Zulus on a night raid. He slowed them to a walk again, holding his stick high and examining the bush around them carefully, more for the pleasing effect of being in charge than because he expected any danger. And then they were off again with the cool, night wind in their faces.

'He-he-Hey!'

'Ja man, *lekker*.'[1]

They lay on their stomachs in the pumpkin field and Fan told the dogs to be still. The porcupine took so long in coming that they were nearly asleep by the time it appeared. Suddenly Mponyane felt Ting-a-ling's fur stiffen under his hand. A low vibration in the dog's throat told the boy that it had seen something. Mponyane poked Fan awake with one of his sticks.

'He-he! He-he!' he whispered.

'What's it man?'

Mponyane made the porcupine with his hands. It was there, as real as the beast that snuffled in the weeds, and Fan knew at once what to expect. Boelie was on her feet now, staring out into the darkness and Fan took hold of her collar. And then, into a clear patch of moonlight, came *two* porcupines, the biggest Fan had ever seen.

'Wow, Mponyane! They're huge!'

The battle of the porcupines didn't last long – but it was exciting while it was happening. The dogs could not be restrained any longer and dashed out from their hiding place at full bark, closely followed by the two intrepid hunters brandishing their hunting sticks. Mponyane felt a surge of joy. This was the way to live!

The porcupines bristled into two bushes of needles. The dogs pounced. The dogs leaped backwards about twice as far as they had just come, vowing to themselves never to attack these stupid creatures

[1] great

41

again, and the porcupines beat a hasty retreat back into the safety of the long grass, vowing to themselves not to bother with pumpkins for a while. It was all very satisfying. And there were dozens of quills to pick up as mementoes of the mighty battle. It was great. The impi made their way homeward with quills stuck into their hair and sticks over their shoulders at a jaunty angle.

It was soon after that when Kra decided that something should be done about Mponyane. He had been with them for two months now and it was hard to imagine a time when he hadn't been part of their lives. He had his own ideas about how things should be managed, did Mponyane. He had brought his mattress in to sleep near Frank's bed as if protecting him from danger. Mubi had been right when he brought Mponyane to them, Kra decided, and maybe he had been wiser than Kra had realized at the time. Mubi noticed things. A lot more than Kra knew. She had thought that they would be helping Mponyane. Now she saw that Mponyane was helping them. It was strange that such a young boy could understand so much. He didn't need to speak, she sometimes thought. His eyes spoke for him and he always seemed to know when one of them was unhappy.

It was some time before Kra realized what was so very different about Mponyane. It wasn't that he was deaf or that he didn't speak, these were just the characteristics one noticed first because they were more obvious. The unusual thing about Mponyane was that he gave. He looked at Cecily when she came home from school on a Friday afternoon and he saw that she was tired and low, so he brought her some little white stones for her collection, or a flower that had struggled somehow through the drought. He watched over Frank and cared for him like an anxious mother hen with a chick and for Kra herself he had a special understanding on the days when the farm and the work and the worries about money just became too much for her to bear. He brought something new into the lives of all of them, and it was good.

But what would happen when Frank began to grow up? After the summer he would have to go to school – and what would Mponyane think about that? The idea began to grow in Kra's mind that perhaps there was a school for Mponyane too. A school where he could be taught to deal with his deafness. The first step was to have his hearing tested. Properly, by a doctor in a clinic with the right equipment. And the nearest clinic was the one at the mine, where Kra did not wish to go. Did not wish to go – but would go.

It was an expedition. There was not much money, but Mponyane could hardly go dressed as he was in faded, patched shorts and an ancient T-shirt proclaiming the delights of Pepsi in barely legible letters. With a sigh Kra dug into the small savings they still had and bought red shorts and blue socks and white *tackies*.[2] There was an unexpected hitch when Mponyane refused to wear his new blue socks unless Frank had some too, but Cecily came to the rescue with a pair of hers that had shrunk in the wash. Nobody could have been more proud than Mponyane when he and Fan and Kra climbed into the truck for the drive to the mine compound. He was like a peacock with new tail feathers. The two boys giggled and poked each other in the ribs and kicked against the seat until Kra had to be quite sharp with Frank.

'Tell Mponyane to be quiet!' she snapped, and then was sorry she had been so harsh when the boys

[2] Trainers

went to the other extreme and sat silent all the rest of the way.

The mine hadn't changed. The same security guard – he remembered her of course – and the same red and white striped boom over the gate. The same dirty grey buildings and the same background hum of heavy machinery.

Kra turned the truck into the entrance to the clinic and parked neatly in front of the door. She took a deep breath.

'Come on boys,' she said.

The doctor was young, new; didn't know them.

Kra sat in front of his desk with one boy on either side of her and her handbag clutched firmly on her lap.

'This child is the son of a miner who worked here for many years.' Kra told the surprised looking doctor. 'He's dead now but, since it was the mine-dust that killed him, I think the management owes it to this boy to see if anything can be done.'

'Er . . . yes, well . . . let's have a look at the young man.' The doctor seemed rather at a loss and took refuge in professional procedure. He looked carefully into Mponyane's ears and sounded various things that looked like forks close to his head. Frank covered his own ears at the high pitch of some of them, but Mponyane did not react. The doctor put some headphones on Mponyane and fiddled with a tape recorder for a while. Mponyane sat still and quiet, occasionally looking round to see if Fan was still there. At last it was finished.

'Well Mrs, er . . .'

'Saunderson.'

A flicker of surprise passed over the doctor's face. 'Yes, well, Mrs Saunderson. I'm afraid that this child is profoundly deaf. That means,' he added in explanation, 'that he can hear almost nothing. From what

44

you tell me this is probably as a result of measles shortly after he was born.'

'And what can be done?' Kra asked quietly. The doctor had, after all, only confirmed what they already knew.

The young man spread his hands in a gesture of hopelessness.

'Very little, I'm afraid.' He glanced at Kra and Frank. Shabby, that's what they were. Not much money there. 'There are very few schools for deaf ... er, African children.' He averted his eyes tactfully. 'And the schools are, ah ... quite expensive.'

He was relieved when there was a brisk tap at the door. He wished this woman and her problem would get out of his clinic and leave him in peace.

'Come!' he called irritably, and then got to his feet quickly as the mine manager entered. Even if Mr Cooper hadn't been the manager, his height and breadth would have inspired respect, he seemed to fill all the space left in the room. He shut the door sharply behind him and turned to the doctor scowling with annoyance.

'Dr Grier, in future I'd like you to ...' Then he broke off abruptly. 'Jean! What the devil are you doing here?'

He looked strange, Dr Grier thought, almost afraid. Now why should someone as arrogant and self important as Bill Cooper look frightened of a woman with two children? He filed that thought away for future reference. One never knew when impressions like that could be useful.

Kra drew herself up to her full height. 'I have brought a child, the son of one of your miners. For testing. His hearing that is.' She seemed flustered, not sure what to say.

'Yes, well ...' The manager had recovered from the shock of seeing her, but he was still uncertain of

45

himself. 'You know Sylvia and I have been meaning ... that is we intended to ...' Then he stopped floundering and seemed to draw his usual dignity back into himself. 'Are you managing? If you have come about any kind of loan, I'm afraid ...'

Kra looked away, out of the window. 'No, I haven't come about any kind of loan. We manage. There is a little income from my Dad's farm – he died you know, six months ago – and Etienne and I had some savings.'

Mr Cooper was relieved. He had been afraid there might be a scene. Weeping woman and children, that sort of thing. 'Well, if there is anything we can do – anything else, that is.' He looked as if he was about to close this unwelcome episode by leaving.

Kra made a sudden decision. 'Yes, there is, as a matter of fact. This child, Mponyane. I can't afford to send him to a special school for the deaf. Would the mine perhaps pay for him? His father worked here for many years, and he and the mother are both dead. The family must surely be entitled to some help.'

The mine manager smiled smoothly. This was familiar ground. People were always asking him for money. 'No, I'm afraid we could hardly do that. Have the whole lot of them after us for the same sort of thing.' He laughed lightly at the thought, then looked at Mponyane reflectively. 'But when he's older I'll see about getting him a job. Sheltered employment. Something even a deaf black could manage. Surface job.' He thought he was being quite generous really.

Kra took them home by way of the village, stopped defiantly at the store and bought the two boys ice creams she could not afford. It helped to make her anger less.

7

Sometimes when Mponyane and Fan were playing, Mponyane had the strangest feeling of being watched. They would be in their secret place, or down at the old sheep-dip, or climbing the gum tree, and Mponyane would look round, expecting to see someone. And there would be nobody. It worried him. Kosie had been keeping out of their way, they had only seen him once in the village, glowering from a shop doorway, but he had not tried to speak to them.

Mponyane was sure that Fan had not forgotten the big redhead either. In the night Fan often thrashed around and kicked off his blankets and Kra sometimes even came in her dressing gown and comforted him. Mponyane was sure that Fan had bad mind pictures of the big boy.

They still practised with the fighting sticks, but after the great porcupine hunt Mponyane had less confidence in Fan's ability. He was only a small boy after all and not very strong. The only answer was to keep close watch and to be ready at all times in case of trouble. Like a real Zulu.

Mponyane wished he had learned more. When he had reached the age of the ear-piercing he had still been with the other boys. He often thought about the party his people had held that night. It had been a big occasion with many boys from the surrounding villages who had reached this important milestone together.

Mponyane had not really understood what was going to happen, but Baba had shown him with signs that he was not to be afraid and had stayed with him until the time. And the ear-piercing had not hurt very much. Mponyane had realized that it was important and that he must show himself to be a man and not afraid. There had been beer and meat afterwards and Baba had given him a new T-shirt, the one he still wore with the red pattern. Some of the other boys had received real white shirts with long sleeves, but Mponyane thought that his present was better because it came from Baba.

But somehow, after the ear-piercing, the other boys had gone from Mponyane. They had never been unkind to him, or hurt him, but he had begun to feel apart. They made rapid mouth movements about things that Mponyane could not understand and went off together into the veld on mysterious missions, without him. Mponyane was glad now that he had Fan and a responsibility in his life. He was an important person, the umtalaan of Fan, and he hefted his fighting sticks more firmly in his hand and peered into the bush as if defying dangers to come at him.

The farm was bone dry and the dust drifted across it in a choking haze when the wind blew. Dark clouds lumbered along the horizon, but no rain fell. There had been none since the day Mponyane arrived at the farm. The *mealies* were dying in the field and the cabbages, which had been planted with such hope, drooped and faded in their furrows. The frown between Kra's eyes deepened and she went even less to the village. Some days they all had *mealie meal* for supper, even Cecy who didn't like it.

Kra's words:

There came a time when there was nothing else to do, but go to Etienne's father for a loan. Even if it rained tomorrow, it would come too late to save my poor crops. One evening I sat with my account books, took a long hard look at our position and decided that I must go to Durban and ask the old man for help.

I doubted if the truck would make the journey, it was held together with bits of string and optimism as it was. I would have to go on the train. I considered taking the children – they were his only grand-children after all – but the extra fares would empty the last of our savings account. Cecily was a sensible girl and nearly thirteen by now, and she would have Mponyane to help her in the house and old Induna to keep an eye on what was left of the farm.

It was a bitter decision to make. I had been so proud, so certain of myself after the trial that I had refused all offers of help. I think I was numb with the shock of it all. I just wanted to escape to Dad's farm and hide from those accusing looks. At the back of my mind were the childish words that Frank often used, 'It's not fair!' And it wasn't. Surely, some-time, all this trouble had to come to an end? There had to be an ending to it, and if I could not believe that, then I could not go on.

Once I had decided, there was no point in waiting. I booked my seat on the train, packed a few things, and called the children and Mponyane in to explain.

'I am going to Grandpa,' I told them, 'to see him about some important business. I know I can trust the two of you to behave while I'm away.'

I remember turning to Mponyane too, like an idiot, and telling him the same thing, only more slowly. Even then none of us, except perhaps Frank, *really* understood what it was like for him. He was so quick, so clever, so caring, that he almost seemed to hear what we said. He certainly understood my every mood. He communicated.

Once when I was going to see the bank manager – and consequently wearing one of my outdated smarter dresses – he took me firmly aside and informed me with his wonderfully clear sign language that, although it was a very pretty dress, the skirt was too short. I was so amused that I actually went and changed. We were used to him, you see. We thought we knew him.

It was sad, leaving the farm, driving the truck to the station through the dried up fields. They'd burned the veld at the end of the winter, waiting for the rain, and the land was black, black like a funeral, and the light pale as a duck's egg and dry too. For the first time in months I felt the tears running down my cheeks and dripping wetly onto my shirt. I was so tired. So tired.

Kra's train had barely pulled out of the station before Kosie struck. He did not know she had gone. He had just been waiting for his chance to hit back at the Saunderson kid and by pure luck it came on the same day.

Kosie had started to watch the Saunderson farm, at first because of Cecily. He liked looking at her and it was something to do in the long afternoons after school – homework was not something that bothered Kosie overmuch. The rest of the gang wondered where he went. He didn't tell them. It gave him, he felt, an air of mystery, like a spy in a film. He *started* because of the girl, but soon he found himself watching Frank instead.

Sometimes Kosie felt that he was two people instead of one. The good part of him wanted to be liked, to be nice to people, but the other part stamped his foot and said, 'No. Why should you? Why should you, Koos van Schalkwyk, be kind to boys who have families and mothers who make them sandwiches for break and sisters who smile sometimes with hair that shines gold in the sun? Why? Why should you be polite, even, to boys who have dogs who follow them with love in their eyes?' Kosie remembered things about a small black dog. Things that hurt. So he turned his anger on the hurt, and blasted it, until only the hard feeling remained.

The good part of Kosie tried to warn him. 'You'll stay like that if you let the hard take over.' It reminded him of something one of his stepfathers had said to him. 'Take that fat lip off your face. The wind will change and you'll stick like that.'

Watching Frank Saunderson, who had everything that Kosie didn't, the wind changed in Kosie's heart. 'I'll show him. I'll get him on his own and I'll beat him so hard, he won't *ever* forget the name Koos van Schalkwyk.' Kosie's hands curled into fists at the thought and he made a plan. First he'd have to get the dogs out of the way, and that black kid. It was a challenge. It gave him something else to think about, outside the circle of his own fears. 'Ja. I've got to get the dogs out of the way.'

So he built a dog trap.

Mponyane was worried. There was something happening, and he couldn't work out what it was. In the time he had been on the farm he had watched and felt everything about the people and the place. He knew Cecy and her soft-heartedness. He knew Kra's worry and her loneliness. He saw the heart of Fan. The dogs were his friends now, and so was Induna, the old man who had been on the farm so long that he would never go, even if Kra could not always give him his money. The women who worked in the fields brought him sweets sometimes and smiled at him always.

Mponyane knew the light of morning and the high heat of midday. He knew the dry feeling when the clouds formed and the water rolled across the sky far above their heads, but no rain fell. He was used to the place now. He thought he understood it.

But Kra had gone. With a small brown box with a handle and some clothes inside it. She had made mouth shapes at Fan and Cecy and her face had been serious and sad. And then she had made more mouth shapes at Mponyane, but slower and with wider mouth openings. Mponyane had tried to look as if he understood, because he wanted to help. But he had not known what she was trying to explain to him. And now it was dark and she had not come home. Mponyane looked at Cecy, but she was making beans on toast for their supper and not paying attention. She looked quiet and a little sad too, but not worried.

Mponyane looked at Fan. He was drawing with his coloured pencils. It was a picture of Mponyane with his fighting sticks, but for once Mponyane was not pleased with this. How could Fan draw when Kra was gone? And then Mponyane noticed that the dogs were missing.

Fan must have realized at the same moment. He stopped drawing and sat up. His face had the face he wore when something was happening that Mponyane could not understand. Sometimes he thought it might be mouth movements that only they could see. They put their heads kind of sideways and a far-looking expression came into their eyes so that they were not seeing you. Fan did this now.

Then he jumped up, looking very worried and made signs to Mponyane. Boelie and Ting-a-ling and Pannekoek were in danger! Mponyane grabbed their hunting sticks – Fan's too because he had rushed out without his – and followed Fan at a run into the darkening farmyard. If Cecy called after them, neither of them heard her.

The two boys ran over the veld towards the secret place. Mponyane easily caught up with Fan and forced the sticks into his hand. If there was danger, he might need them.

8

It was a good dog-trap. It had taken Kosie some time and a lot of hard work to make – so much hard work that he had considered calling the others in to help. But in his heart Kosie knew that this was a really bad thing he was doing. They might have refused and Kosie could not afford to risk that. His leadership of the gang was not exactly beyond question yet.

So he dug on his own, cursing the heat and the dust and the flies that came to lick at the sweat that poured off his body in streams. When the trap was finished he was delighted with the result. It was the best thing he had ever made himself, about six foot deep, square, with smooth, neat sides. Kosie covered it carefully with light branches and handfuls of dry white grass from the scorched veld.

The part of the plan that he was most pleased with was the meat. This had called for advanced planning and thought – something which Kosie was not normally very good at. Not only had he stolen the meat well ahead of time (from the hostel kitchen when Tannie Kerrie was looking the other way) but he had also thought of burying it in a hole, well covered with loose soil, so that the dogs would not smell it before he was ready for them. Now, as he dug the horrible parcel up, he realized how wise this had been. He dropped the meat through a gap in the branches covering the trap, hid himself behind a clump of reeds, and settled down to wait for as long as it took.

He did not wait long. Frank was busy doing something with paper and pencils that did not interest dogs much – and the smell was truly delicious. The three dogs slipped unnoticed from the kitchen and headed for the dam.

Kosie had never been entirely clear about what would happen when the dogs finally came. He supposed that one, or all of them would fall into the pit, putting themselves in his power. He hoped that the Saunderson kid would come looking for them, in the dark maybe, and without that black side-kick. But he hadn't meant to hurt the dogs. Never. He'd *never* meant to do that. And he hadn't reckoned on the screaming.

Boelie was in the lead – Boelie always led – closely followed by the other two. Ting-a-ling's little silver bell jingled along the path somewhere behind, and Pannekoek's white patch shone in the last of the evening light. The clouds still hung over the hills, as they had this past month, and there was an occasional low rumble of thunder, but the dogs paid no attention. They were used to the sound now.

The scent came from the dam, from the place where Frank and Mponyane played. Boelie trotted even faster. It was meat! The dogs had been on *mealie-pap* for weeks now and the saliva dribbled from the corners of their mouths at the thought of meat again.

One moment Boelie was running eagerly along the track, and the next moment the ground disappeared from under her paws and she dropped down into the dog-trap. As she fell she twisted desperately to try and regain the safety of the path, falling awkwardly with her back legs crumpled underneath her brown furry body.

And then the screaming began.

It was like no sound that Kosie had ever heard. It raised the hairs on the back of his neck and on his forearms and left him crouching, frozen with horror in his hiding-place. 'I never meant to hurt the dog,' he whispered to himself, over and over. 'I never meant to hurt the dog.'

And still the dog screamed, on and on. Kosie clapped his hands over his ears, turned tail and ran, blundering through the bushes in the half light with branches scratching and spitting at him, trying to stop him as he fled.

By the time Frank and Mponyane arrived, the screaming had mercifully ceased. Ting-a-ling and Pennekoek were whining at the edge of the pit with terror in their eyes. And Boelie was dead.

They buried her in a place she had loved, a patch of garden where the rose bushes straggled across a broken trellis and there was a shattered stone bird-bath. Cecy brought the blue gaslamp from the kitchen and the cold light flickered eerily over the three children and the two remaining dogs. Not even Frank had tears enough to cry any more. They took it in turns to dig until they thought the grave was deep enough and then lowered Boelie carefully into it, wrapped in her red blanket from the place where she had slept. Mponyane had never felt such sadness as came from Cecy and Fan. It washed from them to him in great waves that brought coldness to his heart. He stroked Cecy's arm softly, looking his compassion for her.

'Heya, Heya,' he repeated. 'Heya, Heya.'

Cecy gave a small smile.

'You don't understand, do you Mponyane?' she said quietly. 'Maybe it's better that you can't hear. Maybe you would hear things that would make you dislike us as well.' She looked at him intently, trying to look into his mind with her words that he could not hear. 'Maybe you would change, Mponyane, if you could hear.'

Mponyane felt her distress from something else, not just Boelie, but he didn't know what caused this other hurt. 'Heya, Heya,' he whispered. It was all he could say.

Sadly the three of them went back to the darkened kitchen. Cecy's toast had burned and the beans were a dried-out mess in the bottom of the pot, but none of them were hungry. Frank went to his room and lay down on his bed with his eyes shut, but he didn't sleep. He couldn't. He heard the sound again and again. The sound of Boelie when she had cried for him to come, and he thought he would never be able to hear anything else ever again.

Cecy smiled at Mponyane, a tired, thin smile that reminded him again of Kra.

'Goodnight, Mponyane. I wish I could explain to you. I wish I could make it right.' She picked up her book and left, her feet dragging a little behind her and her shoulders sagging.

Mponyane wandered outside. There was a bare light-bulb on the back stoep and moths fluttered drunkenly against it. There was a small heap of their bodies lying in the pool of light. In the morning Induna would sweep them up and next evening the survivors would come again. Mponyane sat at the edge of the circle on the cool stone, with his knees drawn up under his chin. There had to be a pattern in what had happened, but he could not see what it was.

Again and again he reviewed the events of a perplexing day and could make no sense of them. Where was Kra? Why was there this hate-feeling around his white family that would not go away? One thing was clear. Fan was at risk, in grave danger. For Mponyane had seen what Fan had not. He had seen the dirty white track-suit top with the three green stripes across the chest. It had been lying near the place where Boelie died. And it belonged to the big red-headed boy who had hurt Fan.

With sudden resolution Mponyane stood up. It was plain to him that the red-boy had made the trap in order to catch Fan. The red-boy wanted to kill his umtalaan and Mponyane was going to stop him because Baba trusted him to look after Fan.

If only he understood more! Everything was getting so difficult now. First in his own place, when the boys went away and he stayed behind, and now here. Life swirled past in a rush and a hurry that left him standing looking vainly after it, smiling hopefully and trying, trying to work out what had happened.

He knew that there was something he should do, something he had seen done in his own place where there had been bad things to make right. Maybe there *was* a pattern after all, Mponyane decided, thinking of the green snake. Yes, that had not been an accident. He shuddered when he thought of it, slithering across the dry earth between the reeds.

Mponyane went to the place where he and Kra had put the snake. Really strong medicine was needed if Fan was to be protected. He didn't think about what he was doing, or about his fear of the snake. He found the bones quite quickly, nearly clean, shining whitely in the overspill of light from the stoep, strange and spiky and delicate.

He washed the biggest one, and left it on some newspaper to dry. Then he carefully made a little bag out of the soft leather from the edge of an old sheepskin he had found in the store. He tied the dry bone into the bag with a thong to hang it around Fan's neck. He realized now that he had been wrong about the green snake. It had obviously been a spirit sent to warn him and he had carelessly ignored the warning. Well, he knew better now. This bone of the great green snake would surely be powerful enough to protect Fan.

Mponyane made a few more preparations. Then he packed his things into his sack, his new shorts and socks, the clay oxen – Fan's as well – and some food. Then he went to wake Fan. It was time for them to leave.

9

There was no starlight at the beginning of this
journey. Only the gleam of a fitful moon glimpsed
between rolling, boiling, black dark. The white line
in the middle of the tar road was sometimes all that
Mponyane could see, and then the big road ended
and there was dirt, and dust that rose with small
puffs at each step. One foot and then the other until
they came to the place where the hills started to
sweep gently down into the valley, and the track was
grassed over. The inner call of Mponyane's home
was sweet and clear.

He had no doubt that he was doing the right thing.
The further they travelled on the road to his home,
the more certain he became. In his *kraal* Fan would
be safe from the red-boy and from whatever the
strange evil was that threatened him from the village
people. When Cecy woke up in the morning, they
would be far from the farm. This was the only bad
thing. What would Cecy think? But Mponyane dis-
missed this quickly from his mind. She had Ting-a-
ling and Pannekoek, who were locked in the shed to
prevent them from following Fan, and she was able
to look after herself. She would go to her friend, a
dark-haired girl Mponyane had seen with her once.
Maybe she was not a real friend, not in the way that
Mponyane and Fan were friends, but at least she had
been talking to Cecy that day and smiling with her

about something. Surely she would help if there was trouble? In truth Mponyane did not want to think about this, so he concentrated instead on the way.

He had not forgotten it. Every turn and twist of it lay deep in his mind from the times he had walked this way with Baba. The smells were the same; remembered. Dust and cows and something else that was unidentifiable, but was the smell of this road, and this place.

Every few paces Mponyane looked round to see if Fan was still following. It had been difficult to wake him and Mponyane was sure he had been having bad mind shapes about Boelie. He was very pale and quiet, but he had understood that there was something urgent that must be done. Fan always understood. He had taken the fighting sticks Mponyane held out to him and trotted along behind as if he didn't really care where they were heading. Maybe he thought they were going to hunt porcupines again. Maybe he didn't think about it all. There was no way that Mponyane could explain either. Fan just trusted him. That felt good.

When the sky began to lighten, Mponyane stopped for a while and showed Fan that he must sit. There was some hard bread that Kra had brought from the village three days ago and five dried up apples. Mponyane had also brought a bottle of water from the tap because there would be no streams running until they reached the mountains. Fan was thirsty and drank most of the water, but Mponyane didn't mind. He would have water later – and it would come from Baba's old brown pot with the chip in the rim, the one he had always drunk from when he had been small. The thought gave Mponyane new energy. He put the left-over food and the empty bottle back into his sack and picked Fan's fighting sticks up with his own. Mponyane could see that Fan was very tired.

For a while they played the shape game. As they walked Mponyane made trees and sheep and insects with his hand and Fan had to point to the thing he had made, but he did it listlessly, as if he didn't really want to play. Mponyane did a little dance, backwards on the track and Fan smiled, but only a little. Mponyane began to wish that Baba was there. Baba would know what to do, and Baba was strong and could maybe carry Fan if his feet were sore. It was worrying to be the one who had to make the decisions with nobody to take charge if things went wrong.

The sun dragged itself up through the livid storm clouds and it was hot. One foot after the other. One foot after the other. They were climbing rapidly now and Mponyane had to stop quite often to let Fan rest. But they were near! Mponyane knew they were near. There was the small water place where the old woman with the humped back kept her ducks. There was the hut that had burned down. There was the wattle plantation. Mponyane's feet went faster and faster, one in front of the other.

'Hey-Hey! Hey-Hey!' He showed Fan with signs that something good was going to happen and Fan nodded as if he understood. Soon they would be there and then everything would be all right.

The herdboys were sitting at the place where the small cows were kept, and Mponyane's heart leaped inside his chest. There was the one with the strange eye, and the one who wore an orange blanket, and the one who had once given him a small spear made of blue-gum wood. There was the one Mponyane thought of as 'Nunu' and the one with the mind shape that was 'Fin'.

'Hey-Hey! Hey-Hey!' Mponyane waved and smiled and grabbed hold of Fan's hand, pulling him forward bodily.

'Hey-Hey!'

The boys looked at each other and then at Mponyane and the small white boy. Fin raised a hand in languid greeting.

'Sawubona Mponyane,' he said. 'Sawubona,' he added, turning to Fan.

'Nisaphila,' Fan said automatically. Fan had spoken Zulu as soon as he could speak English. Maina had taught him. But the bigger boy had a mother who believed in Education, so he had been at school all the way to Standard Three and he wanted to show off his own command of another language in front of his friends.

'Why do you come here with the one who does not speak?'

Fan considered this for the first time. He had been so numbed with grief for Boelie that he had not yet given the matter much thought.

'I don't know,' he said at last. The big boys laughed, but not unkindly.

'Hawu! You have come a long way for one who does not know why he has come!'

Fan squatted down on the ground like the other boys, and Mponyane put his sticks down beside him.

'Ja, man,' he said easily. 'Mponyane just showed me I must come. So I came.'

'This boy is working for your people?' Fin asked in surprise.

Fan turned to smile up at Mponyane. 'Ja. He is my umtalaan.'

'But how can this be? How can you speak with him. How can he hear you?'

'Easy, man. We just know what we want to say. Don't we Mponyane?'

Mponyane was watching closely, turning from one boy to the other. They were making the mouth movements again – quickly – and sometimes both of them

63

did it together. When the people made slow movings, Mponyane could sometimes guess what they meant. Now he couldn't even tell which one was the important one. All the boys laughed, looking at Fan.

'Heh-Heh-HEY!' Mponyane joined in, and they laughed and smiled again, and Mponyane thought that it was good to be back with his friends. They had sour milk and *mealie pap* which they were happy to share, and Fan looked brighter, less pale, after he had eaten the food.

At first it was good just to rest. Mponyane sat cross-legged on the ground letting the sun warm him and the responsibility slip from him. He realized how tired he was.

They must go to Mubi of course, but there was no hurry. Baba would be busy in his *mealie* patch or with his vegetables and there was not the need to rush, rush, rush here in the mountains as there was in the valley. Deep contentment came over Mponyane. Here they would be safe. Here Fan was with his friends and all would be well.

But soon Mponyane began to wonder if these were *really* his friends. He began to remember how it had been before Baba took him to Kra, and he began to feel once again the loneliness of his silent world. Fan had slipped into a kind of easy companionship with the other boys almost at once. Because they all had the mouth movements. Mponyane, as usual, was on the outside of the group. He sat up straight again, concentrating on what was happening.

For a moment he closed his eyes, wishing that he did not have to work so hard to understand. He was so very tired now. They liked Fan, he could see that at once – and understood it, because he too had liked Fan on that first meeting. They wanted to show off a bit. And they were bored. It was hot and dry and the cattle were standing dully in the long dry grass chewing the tasteless stalks without enthusiasm. There was nothing to do.

There was some more rapid mouth moving between the boys. Fan joined in a little, but mostly he sat quietly. Mponyane watched, desperately trying to understand what was happening. They were all standing up. Mponyane stood up as well. Fan smiled and touched his arm. He stood right in front of Mponyane as he had learned to do, and made the mouth movement that Mponyane knew.

'Dam,' he made. Mponyane grinned. He knew what that meant. He stood up and started to lead the way to the dam.

Fan turned back to the other boys. 'See. It's easy.'

They were suitably amazed.

Swimming needs no language. The dam, like the one on the farm, had shrunk to a smaller, muddier version of itself, but there had been rain in the mountains and a small trickle of brown water still ran through. Mponyane felt the coolness of the water. It seemed to soak in through his skin and soothe him.

Nunu pushed Orange-blanket and he, in turn, ducked Nunu. Fin splashed Fan and he dived under the water and tipped Fin under. Mponyane slipped and fell on the slimy bottom and everyone laughed – including Mponyane – and when they were tired they lay in the deep, black, midday shade of a thorn tree and chewed stalks of grass, and watched the cattle drift across the veld, and studied the massive clouds that were building up again behind the mountain.

In that moment of rare comradeship Mponyane was almost sure that he had done the right thing; almost sure.

10

Kra's words:

I knew at once where they had gone. Cecily was waiting for me at the station.

'I tried to get you at Grandpa's, but you'd already left. I didn't tell him . . . I didn't think you'd want me to.'

Poor child.

'I haven't been to the Police or anyone either . . . the boys will probably be back today in any case . . .' And then she burst into tears.

There were a few curious looks, but nobody came over to ask if they could help. I put my arm round Cecily and led her out to where I'd parked the truck. Then, when she'd stopped sobbing, I got the whole sad story – about poor Boelie and the dog-trap, and the grave they had made, and about how she had found Frank and Mponyane gone the next morning, but had only started to worry by lunch time and hadn't been able to reach me in Durban. She had walked all the long, hot way from the farm to the station so that she could tell me the news as soon as I arrived. I felt again the loneliness of being without friends. There had been nobody for her to turn to. We sat in the stifling hot cab of the truck, my arms round my daughter, and despair in my heart.

Somehow the big things are easier to cope with. Like the day of the accident when the sirens wailed through the whole village and the smoke rose from the minehead and every soul in the place walked in dread about their men. That day I had been calm, collected, every inch the mine manager's wife. I'd stood at the pit head handing out hot coffee to the rescue workers and sympathy to the wives waiting for news of their husbands.

It was the same on the day Etienne came home early and told me he'd been suspended until the results of the accident inquiry came out. I hadn't cried then, or become hysterical. I just made him a cup of tea and listened quietly. Gross negligence, they called it and there was talk of funds which had been taken. Money which should have been used to buy safety equipment. Although my brain had registered how serious this was, my heart had been calm. I knew my Etienne. I knew there was a mistake.

There was a mistake all right. Somebody had done those things, somebody had taken that money. The Judge decided it was my husband. And sitting with Cecily, listening to her shuddering breath when she had finished crying, I felt only bitterness at the injustice of it all.

We packed food and a first aid kit from the kitchen. I fed Ting-a-ling and Pannekoek. They were still subdued and quiet, wagging their tails when they saw me, but with nervous little wags almost as though they expected to be beaten. I did not go and look at Boelie's grave. That would come later. Cecily put the sleeping bags in the truck too, and some pillows for the boys to lie on – when we found them.

'They will be with Mubi?' she kept saying anxiously. I told her I was sure that they would be. Where else could they go?

We set off towards the mountains in the threatening late afternoon. When would the rain come again?

Black, black the burned veld stretched away on either side of us and the heat haze shimmered the hills into distorted waves.

'They will be with Mubi?' Cecily asked for the twentieth time.

'Yes. They will be there.'

Please, God, let them be there.

The heat beat down on the mountains, a hand heavy on a drum, and the waiting veld shuddered under it. When the sun's rays were long and slanting and the shadows blackened the cracks and crevices in the hills, the herdboys began to gather the cattle and goats together to drive them to the village. Fan helped enthusiastically. This was the first time he could remember having been part of a group which was not intent on hurting him. Briefly he thought of Koos and his gang. Later, when he had absorbed all the things these boys knew about fighting, he would take them back with him and he would be in the lead. They would take the hostel by storm – Mr Kruger notwithstanding – and show Koos van Schalkwyk a thing or two. Wouldn't they just.

During the long, hot afternoon Fan learned a lot. The herdboys knew more than Mponyane because they had been through the mysterious process of initiation where boys learned to be men. Of course they could not tell him all that happened when they went away, such knowledge was, he must understand, too dangerous.

'These things, they are not for children,' Nunu said gravely. 'This Mponyane, he could not come because he cannot hear.'

'But that's not fair!' Fan protested.

Fin looked at him kindly. 'But how could he know the stories which we have been told if his ears are closed to them? There are many of them – too many to show with signs.'

Fan thought about this for a moment. Mponyane's deafness had never been a problem between them, so he had not seen it as a problem for others. But this was Mponyane's home! He should be part of everything here.

'What will happen to him?' Fan asked quietly. 'When he is older?'

Nunu shrugged. 'I do not know. Maybe he will stay with the women and the old people, but he cannot come with us when we go to the cities to find work.'

Fan remembered Mr Cooper at the mine and his words that had made Kra so angry. 'Surface job,' he had said. 'Something even a deaf black could manage.' Well, Mponyane wasn't a deaf black, he was Fan's friend.

'When I'm big I'll have a farm of my own and Mponyane can come and live in my house and help me!'

This seemed to Fan like a thing that could happen. He would make it happen.

Nunu smiled again. 'Perhaps.'

But Fan could see that he didn't really believe it would be that way at all.

The cattle were listless with heat and poor grass and no trouble to chase home, but the goats were skittish and there was much laughter as Fan tried to round them up with his fighting sticks. One of the boys made him a small shield out of bark and plaited grass and Fan took off his shirt to be more like the others. He wished he had some coal. That would have finished off the job.

But he still managed to look almost like a herdboy by the time they reported to Mubi's hut. Mubi had been tending his small *mealie* patch. Women's work, but there were no women of his family. The young ones had gone to Durban to work as nurses and domestics and the old ones were dead. But water still had to be carried from the tap the headman had got from the Government for them, and the caterpillars and bugs still had to be removed along with the weeds.

He straightened wearily, easing his aching back. Everything was different. Everything had changed. It was the fault of the rains, some said. No, it was the Government, others thought. It was the new ideas the people had got from the mines and the cities, or it was the young people who no longer had respect for their elders. Who really knew? The old ways had gone for good and would never come again.

Mubi scraped the earth from his hoe on a flat stone. It was time to stop now. He squinted up at the rain clouds. Maybe tonight they would have the rain they needed so badly. Every day for weeks he had carried water to trickle over the roots of the mealies and this rain was long overdue.

Someone was calling out. Someone who . . . No! It couldn't be.

'Heya! Heya! Heya! Heya!'

It was Mponyane.

Something had happened, this much was clear, and the something was bad, but Mponyane could not explain. Mubi recognized the anguish in the child's eyes, but he could not help him. Instead he made Fan sit down quietly and tried to find out what had made them run away from the farm.

'Your mother . . . she is sick?'

'No, Baba, she has gone to my grandfather to ask for money.'

Mubi nodded. He knew of the problems with money. Money was slippery. It fell through the fingers like water and was gone. For a woman alone with two children this was bad.

'Why did you come to my home?'

A cloud passed over the child's face. 'They killed my dog. Mponyane and Cecily and I made a grave for her. Then Mponyane showed me that we must go – I think he was afraid something bad would happen to me if we stayed.'

Again Mubi nodded. 'These people ... how did they kill your dog?' This was indeed a bad thing.

Fan's voice wavered, but he told the story of the dog-trap. Mubi was shocked. He knew what was said in the village in the valley, and he did not approve. But to speak was one thing, to act against children was quite another.

'And you told no one that you were coming to me?'

'No, Baba.'

'Your mother will worry.'

Fan had not yet thought of this. He realized now that he should have done so.

'And your sister.'

'Yes.'

Mubi sighed. Suddenly he felt too old to deal with such problems. In his mind he remembered the time when Fan's mother had been young. The time before her marriage when her father had still run the farm and the sweet green mealies stood tall and proud and the women sang as they worked. Was it only because he was old that his mind saw that there had been good rains always and the harvest had been a fine thing to see? Now his eyes saw only dust.

Fan's mother had come to them in the *kraal* one summer because, she said, she wanted to learn their way. She had been so young. Mubi remembered with affection how she had stood before the headman and begged to be allowed to work with the women.

71

'I am tired of the ways of my people,' she had said. 'I would see how your people live, and I want to learn.'

The headman had suppressed his smile, because she was young and earnest, and had allowed her to stay for a summer.

But that had been long ago. Now everything had changed. Mubi looked at Fan again. There was more of his father than his mother in that square chin and those eyes. And he could not stay.

'I must take you back, child. You cannot stay here.'

Mubi smiled at Mponyane, and spoke to him although he knew the boy could not understand.

'I am not angry. You did what you thought was right.'

'Heya, Heya.'

Baffled, Mubi turned away. What was to be done for Mponyane? He began to gather the things they would need and set out some mealie porridge and milk which the boys attacked as if they had seen no food for a week. While they ate, the old man thought. Soon it would be dark and there was no point in setting out now. Besides, Frank was obviously tired out after his long walk and he was a sickly child who should be gently cared for. They must sleep here tonight and at first light Mubi would take them back.

The old man settled the children and they soon slept. But he sat for a long time, looking into the black storm clouds, deep in thought.

High in the mountains behind him the thunder rumbled and groaned. Lightning flashed, baring the rocks and stones to its icy light. And the rain began.

11

Kosie was the only person who saw the truck pull out of the farm road and start along the dusty road toward the mountains.

He was unable, really, to keep away from the farm. His good half dreaded being caught and found out. The other part of him derived a curious kind of satisfaction from the danger. He had told no one about the affair of the dog. He was trying to forget it. But he couldn't.

Last night he had hardly slept and when he did drift off, he was awakened again and again by the sound the dog had made when it was in the trap.

Once Kosie had owned a dog. It had been a small black pup, about six months old and he had loved it. But his real dad had come to the flat one night, drunk and looking for Ma, who wasn't at home, and had smashed the dog against the outside wall and killed it. Kosie had never allowed himself to love anything else.

He tried hating instead, like hating the Saunderson boy. Frank hadn't even known who Kosie was when Kosie had started to hate him. Frank had never done anything to him. Frank had never beaten him, or kicked him or jeered at him. Kosie's two step-fathers had done all of those things, but somehow he had never expected anything else from them. After all, they hadn't asked to have him had they?

He'd just sort of tagged along with his Ma. Kosie felt a bit sorry for them really. Neither of them had been exactly happy with Ma – she'd been out too much for that to happen – and he supposed that thrashing him had given them something to do from time to time.

It had been after he started going with the bigger boys that the trouble had really started. With the Police and that. And when he'd been caught smoking some pot one of the Standard Eight's had given him for a laugh, then he'd felt the heavy hand of the Law all right. 'Place of Safety' the Magistrate had said, with a dirty look at Ma when he said it. 'Boy needs to be properly cared for.' So Kosie was taken away from the grubby flat where his latest step-father lounged on the latest furniture, the stuff that hadn't been taken back by the shop yet. The lady from the Welfare had helped him get his sleeping bag and rucksack into her old Beetle and he'd left home.

And that was how he'd ended up in this rubbish old hostel in the back of beyond, otherwise known as northern Natal. Kosie had expected to be the centre of attention – had been quite looking forward to it in fact, but nobody was really that much interested. He'd arrived just after the accident in the mine when the whole school was still reeling under the shock of it all.

Two of the boys in his class had lost fathers and one an older brother. They had walked in a kind of aura of sympathy and everyone spoke near them in lowered voices. Even old Kruger was nice to them and the women teachers cried over them and let them off their homework. There had been a strange suppressed kind of atmosphere over the whole school and even kids who hadn't lost a relative had done badly in their exams.

And then the whole inquiry business blew up and

74

everyone was talking about how Mr Saunderson had creamed off the money for the safety equipment which hadn't been there when the men needed it. The real tragedy had faded into the background in comparison with this new scandal.

The village had been united in anger as much as it had been in sorrow. With the deaths had come helplessness; now they wanted action. There was ugly talk, talk of retribution, of taking the law into their own hands and dealing with Saunderson themselves. Kosie had listened and watched, wondering at the power of the feelings that swept through a group of ordinary, decent people. The women had been the angriest. If they'd had their way, Etienne Saunderson would have been hung, drawn and quartered – or worse. The under side of everyone's emotions had come to the surface for a while. People stood on street corners, or in the shops, and talked about it with a guilty thrill, as though they were all listening to something that was not really meant for their ears. Kosie had found it all quite fascinating; horrible, but fascinating.

Cecily had been kept out of school for a bit, though she had to come back eventually, but that little creep Frank had managed to get himself put back a year and missed everything. That angered Kosie too.

Kosie liked being angry. It helped him to forget things. But there wasn't as much to be angry about at the new school, because people were kind to him in an absent-minded way, and tried to help him, which Kosie found bewildering and difficult to understand.

He'd heard old Kruger and Mr Ross, the Principal, discussing him when he was supposed to be at soccer practice and he knew what they had been told about Ma. It wasn't fair really. Ma wasn't *that* bad. Maybe

75

she didn't fuss around with food and stuff like other mothers did, but she didn't hit him much, and she sometimes gave him ten rand notes, when she had money. She wasn't soft, Kosie didn't like it when people were soft.

It was easier when people hit you and swore at you, because then you knew where you stood. You could swear back and you didn't have to care about them. This new gentleness in his life was hard to put up with, so Kosie kept his anger warm by thinking about the Saunderson boy who ought to be punished because he had a bad father. Frank became a kind of symbol for the unhappiness of Kosie.

He crouched in the bushes beside the farm road and watched the two in the truck. They were looking pale and frightened, he noticed. Cecily had tied back her long hair with an elastic band, which was a pity because Kosie liked looking at her hair. He sat at the back of the class, so he watched her sometimes when he was supposed to be doing Maths.

They'd shut the other dogs up in a shed. He could hear them whining and scratching to get out and thought, with a pang, that maybe they'd been locked up to stop *him* getting at them. It made him feel bad, that did.

Saunderson's mother drove the truck carefully through the rickety gate and Cecily got out to shut it behind them. There was a lot of stuff piled in the back, Kosie noticed, like they were going on a camping trip maybe. The truck didn't sound too good. One of Kosie's step-fathers had been a mechanic. Kosie knew what sounded right and what didn't, and that truck had a lot wrong with it. He watched them down the farm road, a white triangle of dust stretching back towards him until they disappeared in it and were gone.

It was kind of quiet on the farm after that. Kosie threw a few stones at some ducks, but nobody came out to shout at him. Wasn't much of a farm – anybody could see that, even Kosie who knew a lot more about cities and smoke and crowds than he did about chicken mess and cabbages. Everything looked dead, like it had never really had a chance. The fence posts sagged and the wire was rusty.

He peered in through the kitchen window. Nobody. Where was the Saunderson kid? There was an old chair near the Aga stove with a patchwork cushion. He thought Saunderson's Ma might sit there in the evenings, knitting maybe. Cecily would do her homework at the old table and the kid would lie on the floor playing with some toys. Strange how clear that picture was. As if he'd really seen it before.

Funny Frank wasn't around. And then Kosie began to piece together the parts of the puzzle that he had seen. The shock on Frank's face and the fear on the black boy's, when they had come running up to the dog-trap, the worry he had noticed in Frank's mother and Cecily, the sleeping bags and camping stuff in the back of the truck that had left the farm and turned in the direction of the mountains.

They'd run away! The bloody fools had run away and Cecily and her Ma had gone to look for them.

Kosie didn't feel like hanging about after he'd thought these thoughts, in fact he felt a bit sick and the small, cold voice of his good bit was beginning to speak to him.

'Your fault,' it was saying, 'your fault.' He turned angrily away from the window and started the hot, dusty walk back to the hostel.

Mponyane couldn't sleep. There were too many things in his mind. At first he had thought it was going to be all right, when they got to his place and the herdboys were friendly. He had seen that they liked Fan and that Fan liked them, and for a while his heart had been quiet and his thoughts had been still. Maybe here would be a place where Fan could be safe and well.

But Mponyane was older now that he had been before the green snake and the dog-trap, and some of the things which he had not allowed inside his head before had crept in and would not let him rest. His place and Fan's were different. His people and Fan's people were different. Was there a way for them to cross over?

The ground was hard under his blanket. Mponyane didn't mind, he was used to it. Would Fan even notice that he didn't have a bed to sleep on? Maybe he would think it was fun, a bit of an adventure, for the first week or so, but what then? He would miss his comfortable wooden bed with the pictures stuck on the bed-head from his old birthday cards. Kra had done that for him, every year, so that now the brown wood was covered with brightly coloured scraps of paper; every one a memory.

And what about Kra? Mponyane thought that maybe she had come back from wherever she had gone, and she would be anxious about them. Worries nibbled away at his mind, like small fish. Just when he thought he was going to sleep at last, another one would come along, nibble, nibble. What about Cecy? Maybe that girl, the one with the dark hair, the one he thought might be her friend, had been laughing *at* Cecy, not with her. Maybe Cecy would be afraid on her own in the farmhouse. And what about the dogs? Maybe he should have brought the dogs. And what about Mubi who had been pleased to see them, but also sad and worried. Would he take them back to the farm, or would he allow them to stay? Mponyane sighed and turned over for the tenth time. Why couldn't things have stayed the way they had been?

Kra's words:

At least things were changing. At least something was happening. In a way I had been waiting for this. I was awfully tired of the same thing and all of it bad. Maybe at the back of my mind there was still a little doubt about whether the two boys would be with Mubi, but not much. It was the obvious place for them to go. I knew, because I had done the same thing myself once.

Mubi's people must have thought I was mad! I was eighteen when I decided that western civilization wasn't for me. Luckily Dad was wise enough to give me my head. I suppose he thought I'd soon get sick of sleeping on the hard ground and carrying all that water up from the river. But it wasn't those things that got to me in the end. It was just a feeling of being tolerated by people who liked me for myself, but expected me to leave someday. Ja, it was that feeling that got to me in the end. I was happy enough, and they were fond of me, I know they were, but it wasn't really my place.

Driving was difficult because the road hadn't been graded for ages. The clouds were piled higher than I'd ever seen them, and blacker. With our luck it would probably rain at last, just when we didn't want it.

Cecily was talking more than usual. She's never been a chatterer, but I realized on the drive that she'd been bottling a lot up. I suppose I should have seen it before, but there was always so much to do, so much to think about. You get to a level of tiredness where you just seem to exist and not think much. And Cecily's the kind of kid who would do anything rather than be a nuisance. The kind that always seems to be older than they really are, except for now and again when they break down a bit and you see that they are still children after all.

'Ma,' Cecily said suddenly out of a small silence, 'can't we go and live somewhere else?'

There wasn't much answer to that one. If I could have left this place behind after the trial, I'd have been long gone. Long gone. But I married Etienne straight out of school. No training means no jobs. The only thing I knew was farming – and I wasn't much good at that. At least it was a roof over our heads, and we wouldn't starve as long as there were a few vegetables.

'Maybe we will.' I told her, surprising myself. 'Maybe we'll go and find a new place.'

I'd worry about that one when we found the boys and got them home.

It was tiring keeping my eyes on the road and the ruts in it and the treacherous ridges of soft dust that slid the car across the surface when you weren't expecting it. I found myself thinking that I wouldn't mind too much if I just slipped gently over the edge into oblivion. That's the worst thing I've ever thought in my entire life, that was, even if I did qualify it a bit by imagining that Cecily jumped out before we went over. But somehow there didn't seem to be a lot to look forward to just then. Tired, I suppose. That's what I was.

The mountains were red against the black sky by then, red with the glow of a late and angry sun. I've lived in northern Natal all my life and I've never seen a sky like that. I think it was about then that I began to feel frightened. It didn't happen suddenly. It began more or less the time that the sun started to go, when I had to switch on the lights and the dust danced in their beams. We lost a bit of our exhaust just then, not that it was much of a loss – the thing had been hanging off for months – but the noise was different. It didn't sound like our truck any more. Cecily started to cry then too, so it wasn't just me. I had the feeling that the two of us would go on for ever, driving against that black and red sky. The rain would never fall, and we would never find Frank and Mponyane, and there would never be an end to it; never.

Mubi went inside the hut which was hot and stuffy and smelled of paraffin from the stove and of blankets. Mponyane was asleep again, at last. The old man had heard the child turning in his half sleep, but what could be done? There were no words to be spoken, and no words to be heard. Slowly the old man got ready for sleep, laying his clothes carefully beside his bed and filling the tin mug with water in case he was thirsty in the night. He settled himself neatly on top of the blanket and lay as he always did, staring up at the roof of the hut and thinking about what would come tomorrow. Usually he knew what it would be. The cattle would be dipped at the tanks, or the mealie patch would be hoed, or the headman would come to speak about the water pipe and the people who forgot to turn the tap off so that there was mud all around the stand pipe and the water was wasted. But tonight Mubi didn't know what was going to happen, and tonight he was afraid.

12

There had been talk in the village lately. At the Women's Institute meetings, or in the main street on Friday mornings when the farmers had to go to the bank, the Saunderson family came in for a lot of comment. This was a small community. Jean Saunderson might think she was alone in the world and that nobody knew or cared what became of her, but in fact there was very little that happened out there on the farm that was not known and discussed.

'I see she's got that deaf kid living in the house now.' Nobody had to ask who 'she' was.

'Ja, well she always was thick with the blacks. Lived up there for a while when she was younger. Her old man must have been mad to let her do it, but then he was always over friendly with them as well.'

'Extension officer tells me they've lost the cabbages again.'

'Well . . . without a man on the place . . .'

There was a small silence.

'I never understood about Etienne. Why did he do it?'

'*Did* he do it?'

People began to look away from each other when the name Saunderson was mentioned. They would never forget what had happened. Time would be measured, for everyone who had lived here then, in terms of before and after the disaster on the mine.

No, they could not forget, because nothing would bring back the faces that were missing, nothing would take away the sadness. But there was another part of the business that they wished they could ignore, and that was the turning of the village against Etienne Saunderson.

'Look, it had to be him. Who else had access to the safety fund?'

'Ja, but it wasn't a thing the man would have done. We all knew him before.'

'Well why didn't you stick up for him before?'

There was no answer to this.

Predictably it was the new headmaster's wife, Lisa Ross, who first spoke up in public. She was young and she was new and she didn't understand the way people who had always lived here thought. It was inconceivable to her that people could be so plain nasty to another human being. Surely if someone just pointed out to them that they were wrong . . .

She chose her moment carefully. There had been a cookery demonstration – not that there was a woman in the place who didn't know how to make *koeksisters*, but it was something to do, and there were samples to eat afterwards, and the chance of a good gossip. At least they expected that there would be, although none of them would have actually used the word. 'Discussion' was a more acceptable alternative. And sooner or later in the afternoon the subject of the discussion would be Jean Saunderson.

Lisa Ross put a stop to all that. She was chairlady this year, mostly because her husband was headmaster. Lisa sometimes felt that she didn't have an identity of her own. She was just the headmaster's wife, but she did have a little wooden gavel to bang and they did have to listen to her.

'Ladies! Ladies!' she called them to order. The

buzz of conversation, which had already begun, died reluctantly away. She waited until there was silence.

'There is something which I should like to bring to your attention.' For a moment she looked out of the window. It was difficult to know how to put such a delicate matter. The sight of Bill Cooper's Mercedes roaring past in a cloud of dust hardened her resolve. He was one of the worst.

'It's about Jean. Jean Saunderson,' she added, as if anyone might be in doubt. 'I'm worried about her, out there on the farm on her own, and I think it's time that we as a community forgot our differences and did something about the situation.'

The silence was oppressive. Mrs Elliott rose stiffly to her feet and left without a word. Her husband had lost a leg in the accident. Lisa could feel the rest of her audience slipping away from her as well. This was something they didn't want to hear.

'Look,' she went on desperately, 'it wasn't *Jean* who took the money! She's been punished enough for something she didn't do.'

Some of the women looked away, but nobody spoke. In silence they gazed at her across the expanse of table, decorated with one of Mrs Fraenkel's cross-stitched cloths.

'Please.' Her voice came out as a whisper. Who was she pleading for? Herself or Jean Saunderson? She could feel the tears behind her eyes. The head-master's wife was about to make a fool of herself.

'Well, I'm going to see her. Alone, if I have to.' She stood up and stumbled blindly through the red plastic chairs and the faces she could no longer see.

When she was safely outside, she leant against the wall and pounded her fists against the cool stone, until they hurt.

'I wish I'd never come. I wish I'd never come to this awful place.' And then, suddenly, she was angry.

'Get going, Mrs Headmaster,' she said aloud. '*Do* something for a change.'

Inside the hall, the roar of her car's engine sounded like an exclamation mark at the end of what she had just said. The women quietly put away the chairs and silently went home.

Lisa slowed down once she was out of the village. The road was treacherous after the long drought. She took a few deep breaths and tried to calm down. But she was still angry. She didn't even see Kosie trudging back down the road from the farm, and she wouldn't have cared if she had. Suddenly it was important to do something about righting this stupid situation, before it was too late.

But they weren't there. The truck was gone and the screen door on the stoep banged dismally against its frame, blowing in the wind that had come from the mountains in the last hour. Lisa looked anxiously in that direction, realizing for the first time how threatening the sky was. Suddenly she was tired of everything. When they had come to the village she had been full of sympathy, full of compassion, but it all seemed to have evaporated in the face of the bitterness around her.

It wasn't much of a farm, she thought, looking around her absently. Last time she had come she had been too overwrought to pay much attention to her surroundings. She'd seen Jean Saunderson in the village. It was impossible not to feel sorry for her – and to admire the way she held her head high and ignored the whispers and stares. She had swept into the co-op with her two children and a small African boy, placed her order and left with hardly a word spoken to her. The whole scene had stayed in Lisa's mind until she had felt compelled to do something about it. It took a week to pluck up the courage, but eventually she'd phoned and asked to come out to the farm in her capacity as the wife of the head-master. Once she was there, she'd reasoned, the barriers would break down.

It hadn't worked out that way. All the time she had been wanting to say what was really in her mind. She'd even planned it on the drive out.

'Look,' she had intended to say, 'I know you need a friend, and to tell the truth I'm on my own a lot myself with Paul working so hard – this is his first post as headmaster – and I thought we might talk.'

Or maybe she would just say what was true. 'I'm lonely and unhappy. Please help me!'

But she had said none of those things, had felt an intruder into somebody else's life. They had talked about the drought and the new school hall and the enrolment for the class Frank would join next year, and neither of them had said what was on their minds and in their hearts. Words were so useless sometimes.

The door banged again, reminding her of where she was. It was getting late and soon the light would go. Well, there wasn't much point in hanging around. This would be just another failed initiative, just another wasted attempt to help somebody. Slowly she walked over to the car and started the journey home.

This time she did notice Kosie, trudging along in the eddies of dust and dead leaves whipped up by the wind. She was so discouraged that she almost drove past, pretending that she hadn't seen him. It would have been easier. But she stopped the car and leaned over to open the door for him, summoning a smile from somewhere.

'Hello Koos. Would you like a lift back to the hostel?'

He looked at her without much interest, but he

nodded and got into the passenger seat. She was shocked to see how much he had changed. He'd never been a healthy looking child in spite of all the good feeding he'd had since he arrived, but now he was pale and drained. He looked beaten. In fact, if this hadn't been Kosie the tough guy from Durban, she would have thought he'd been crying.

'Do you want to tell me about it, Kosie?' she said gently. Maybe she could help somebody after all.

When he started, the words wouldn't stop. All the things that Kosie had never said, had tried not to think, even, poured out in a rush.

Lisa had to stop the car. She pulled over to the side of the road and listened, appalled, to the story of Kosie. Words, words, words and behind them a sad and frightened child, who had never been seen before. Lisa felt helpless. What was there for her to say? More words? Piles of words, towering over them both and saying nothing. Silently she reached out her arms and held Kosie while he cried. Over his head she watched the dusty road stretching away to nowhere.

When he had stopped crying, Kosie slumped back into his seat, exhausted.

'So you will take me?' His eyes were desperate. 'You will take me to look for them?'

Lisa looked back at the angry black clouds looming over them. 'We'll find them. But first we'll have to get help. There's a storm coming.'

Even as she spoke the first big drops splashed down into the dust and the rain came at last.

The sweet scent of the rain on the dust woke Mponyane. He came awake suddenly as if he had slept a full night, and he knew at once that bringing Fan here had been a mistake. Sometimes he had to think about things for a while before he got everything organized in his mind, but now he saw clearly where he had gone wrong. Baba would take them back to the farm tomorrow and then it would all start again. There would still be the hate-feeling and there would still be the danger to Fan.

For the thousandth time he wondered why. What was threatening Fan? What had anyone done to bring this on a child? And, worst of all, why was he trapped himself in a world of half understanding so that he didn't know how to help? Mponyane realized sadly that he did not laugh as much now as he had done. Those boys who had gone to the veld had come back different from before. Maybe he had been to the farm, instead of to the veld, and maybe he had come back as a man too.

Mponyane raised himself on one elbow and looked over at Fan where he slept. He was only a little boy. He still sucked his thumb when he was asleep. Baba was asleep too, his arms neatly by his sides as he always slept. He looked older when his eyes were closed and his smile was not there. Briefly Mponyane thought about the Baba of Fan, and the wonderful teeth that he took out when he slept. The thought made him smile a little.

But a decision had to be made. Mponyane sat up and pulled his blanket around him, listing the facts in his head. Baba had told him that he must look after Fan, that Fan was his special friend and responsibility. Baba trusted him to do this thing and there must be no hanging back, no failure, because Baba was too old and had too many other problems to think about.

Kra, who was a strong woman and brave, and would have helped with this task, was mysteriously gone. Cecy was too young and could not be expected to shoulder such responsibilities. To Mponyane's knowledge there was no one else. He would have to do this thing on his own.

13

The important thing, Lisa Ross thought on the rest of the drive back, was to stay calm and unemotional. She realized now that she had not been displaying much of either of these qualities lately. She took Kosie into her kitchen and gave him some hot, sweet tea and a couple of Disprins to combat what she was sure was a severe case of shock.

'Wait here,' she told him. 'I'm going to get Mr Ross.'

Paul was marking books in the room he referred to as his study. It was really the spare room.

'Paul?'

Her husband just grunted something about the Inspector coming.

'Paul!' There was a slight edge to her voice now.

There was no reaction. Calm? Unemotional? She picked up a yearly mark book that was lying on top of a pile of books, and cracked it down on the table. The result was satisfyingly loud. Paul jumped in his chair. He was angry, but at least she had his attention.

'There is an emergency – a real emergency – and I would like you to listen to me and help me do something about it.'

Slowly he put down his pen.

'It's the Saunderson family. The boy has run away because of something Koos van Schalkwyk did – I won't go into that now – and Jean Saunderson and her daughter have gone off to look for him. I don't know if you have looked out of your window any time in the last three hours, but there is one hell of a storm brewing in those mountains and Kosie says the bakkie isn't in too good a shape – and I think you should get on to the mine people and get out the rescue teams, because I'm very much afraid that they are going to be needed.' She stopped there, mostly because she had run out of breath.

Suddenly her husband didn't have on his head-master expression, the one he'd been practising since his appointment, and looked just like he used to before Power came to him.

'Oh,' was all he had to say.

But he got on the phone to Bill Cooper at the mine and made the situation quite clear.

'. . . Yes, I *do* think this is an emergency, and I'm asking you for your help. One of my pupils is missing up there – and I don't know if you have looked out of your window in the last three hours, but . . .' He listened for a few moments, then put the phone down rather hard.

'I never did like that man,' he said with some feeling.

But the mine manager was an organizer, nobody had ever tried to deny that. Within half an hour he had his team assembled at the school hall with ropes and stretchers and first aid equipment enough to stock a small shop. The women rallied round as well. There were flasks of tea and soup, sandwiches – anything they could offer.

They were unhappy. Lisa could see that. Unspoken words hung in the air – words again. Mrs Fraenkel came up to Lisa while she was cutting sandwiches and silently pressed her arm. Maybe it was a kind of acceptance. Maybe they wanted to show by their actions that they were sorry about the way Jean Saunderson had been treated. Yes, Lisa decided, they were sorry, but these were words that were better left unsaid.

She carried on, methodically buttering bread, but her thoughts now were with Kosie. As soon as she was finished, she would look for him and make sure he was all right.

Bill Cooper had taken charge as soon as he arrived. Like all the men he was wearing his overalls and hard hat with the light on the front that they used down the mine.

'I've been in touch with the Met office and the forecast's bad; very bad.' He glanced out of the window and closed his eyes briefly. 'I think we are going to have one daddy of a storm. There's a flood warning out and they're standing by all the way down the river. It could be as bad as the big one thirty years ago.'

There were maps and teams and arrangements for radio contact. All the resources of the community were drawn upon.

'Control point will be on the Van Niekerk's place.' Bill Cooper was saying. 'They're the highest farm. We'll get their labourers organized too, chaps who know the mountains.' He looked up at the waiting men. 'Any questions?' There were none. There seldom were when he was in charge.

'Right . . .' he stopped. A tremendous crash of thunder would have drowned his words if he had carried on speaking. The thunder echoed on and on, seeming to bounce back and forth across the valley from one mountain to another. When it had finished he continued. 'Right, it seems to have hit. Let's go!' Silently the men filed out and climbed into the waiting landrovers and bakkies, and there wasn't one of them who wasn't thinking about what it must be like to be lost in those mountains with this particular storm brewing.

In all the excitement nobody thought to look for Kosie, last seen sitting in the headmaster's wife's kitchen, and by the time they did he was long gone, hidden under a tarpaulin in the back of one of the trucks, on his way to try and find Frank and make up for what he had done.

There wasn't much choice about where he could hide Fan, Mponyane thought. He'd been to all the caves in the area and none of them offered much shelter. There was just the one, the place with the strange drawings. That cave was deeper and drier, but it was a lot more difficult to reach and he didn't know if Fan would be able to climb so far. He looked anxiously at the steady rain outside Baba's hut. It was important to make sure that Fan was dry and would not get sick.

Mponyane had the fear feeling again, like when the snake came. It reminded him about the special safe thing he had made for Fan, so he took out the little leather bag with the snake-bone in it and gently tied the thong around Fan's neck.

It was more difficult to wake Fan this time. He was tired after his long day, and not much sleep the night before. But Mponyane persisted. He knew that if he looked sad Fan would be worried, so he made a great effort and put on his smiling face. Fan sat up and rubbed his eyes. Mponyane made the porcupine shape and Fan grinned to show that he understood. Mponyane made three more porcupine shapes and then a whole lot of smaller shapes. Fan's eyes widened.

'Porcupines,' he whispered, 'with lots of babies?'

It was one of his dearest wishes to have a porcupine baby to raise. How had Mponyane known that?

Fan's eyes shone so that Mponyane knew that he had understood. It was a bad thing to tell Fan something that was not true, but maybe, because he was doing this thing for a good reason, they would really see some baby porcupines.

Baba had an old waterproof coat that had been given to him when he worked as a gardener. It hung from the nail behind the door where it had always hung. Mponyane tied it round Fan's neck by its sleeves and buttoned up the front so that Fan was in a kind of coat tent. It looked funny, but at least Fan would be drier when they got to the cave.

Mponyane looked at Baba who slept the sleep of a good man. He had not even stirred. The fear feeling was worse now, much worse. Mponyane wished sadly that he had someone who understood him. Someone he could share his mind shapes with. He and Fan shared some things, but Fan didn't really know what was inside his head. How could he?

Outside, the rain was a shock. The smell of it was different. The dust smell had washed away and now sheets of water swept at them across the compound. Already the ground was soaking and small streamlets were forming into larger puddles. How had this happened so quickly? Fan didn't seem to mind. After the long drought, the rain was a change. He splashed vigorously in his bare feet, turning to grin at Mponyane again, waving his fighting sticks so that rain got in under the raincoat-tent. Should they go back? Mponyane looked hesitantly over his shoulder. After only three or four minutes walking they could not see Baba's hut. The other huts were only a blur behind the pounding rain.

No, he decided. There was nothing for him there. He saw a sudden clear picture of the place and the people who lived there. They were only the people who weren't living somewhere else. The left-overs. If Kra came, or a policeman, or even a black man – if he was young and strong – they would hand Fan over without a word and Fan would be taken back to the farm and the danger.

Resolutely Mponyane walked on into the rain, showing Fan that he must follow. High above them the first long roll of thunder rumbled across the sky. Fan stopped and looked up in alarm. He wasn't frightened of thunder, but he'd never heard any as loud as this. Mponyane just kept on walking.

Kra's words:

We were in a nightmare and I could see no way out of it. That first crack of thunder just about deafened me. It seemed to go on and on until I wanted to take both hands off the wheel and cover my ears. There had been some rain, just enough to dampen the dust on the windscreen so that the wipers made streaks of mud across it, but now the heavens seemed to open. It was as if that thunder roll was a call to battle. The road was instantly soaked and within minutes was running with water.

'Well, it'll keep the dust down,' Cecily said shakily. I was proud of her then.

It must have been about ten minutes later when I took the wrong turning. Rain was driving into the front of the truck with such force that I could hardly see anything. It must have been, although we didn't know it, the point in the road where there is a gentle bend to the left and a road that goes straight. We went left, and it was only when we hit the gate that I realized what we'd done. Well, we didn't *hit* it, but we skidded across the road in a broadside to avoid it, and ended up facing back the way we'd come.

'Nice turning, Mom,' Cecily said with a shaky laugh. I think she realized that she had to keep me calm. But we were facing the right way again and managed to lurch out of the verge. One of the headlights flickered and died. In the light from the other one I looked across at Cecily.

'Sorry love, we'll have to keep going. We can't stay here.'

'You're *sure* the boys will be with Mubi?'

'Quite sure.' But now I wasn't. If only I'd been able to see properly! I'd travelled that road twenty times before, but now visibility was down to practically nothing and the road was like a skating rink. So we went wrong again, and this time I wasn't even sure what I had done. We were on an unfamiliar rutted stretch of road with what looked like small rivers running across it – and the rain looked as if it would never let up. It didn't really matter that we ran out of petrol just then. I don't think the truck would have kept going much longer anyway.

We sat for about an hour, getting steadily more miserable and afraid. The rain didn't slacken in the slightest, it just went on and on drumming against the roof. Lightning slashed across the sky every so often and the noise of the thunder rumbled and roared in our ears.

We hadn't intended to leave the truck. But the water was pouring in through the cracks around the windows and the floor was already swimming with water. What with that, and Cecily's tears, it was about as wet inside as out by the time we'd been there an hour. Both of us began to get the feeling that any kind of action was better than nothing at all. The torch in the cubby hole still worked – amazingly enough – and I knew that both roads in the area led to the kraal anyway, so we set off to find Mubi and the boys.

The Van Niekerk's farm looked like an operations room in a war film. Excitement was running high.

Everyone wanted to help, to be involved – and more than one of the men in the search party had to admit to a vague feeling of guilt. If the village hadn't turned against the Saundersons after the trial, maybe this would never have happened.

'It's like looking for a needle in a haystack,' Paul Ross declared. He'd insisted on joining the rescue party, looking even less like a headmaster in his borrowed overalls and boots. 'They could be anywhere!'

'Ja, man, but they won't be.' Old Mr Van Niekerk had spread out the aerial photographs of the farm that he'd got last year from the Department of Agriculture. There, clearly visible against the sweep of the foothills, was the farmhouse where they now were, and over to the left the spiral pattern of paths around the huts where Mubi's people lived.

'They'll be here,' he stabbed a long finger onto the kraal. 'With Mubi.' He looked up at Bill Cooper, 'Mubi's grandson is Frank Saunderson's umtalaan. He'll be with Frank. Ja, he won't leave the boy.'

'And the woman? And the girl?'

Without hurry the old man traced the roads that led from the village to the mountains. 'There are only two roads they could have come by,' he glanced at his watch, 'and if they left when that child says they did, they should be at Mubi's by now.' He glanced at the stretchers and other equipment, a slight smile on his face. 'So maybe you won't be wanting all that.'

But the smile faded when he looked again out of the window. 'It's the weather you have to worry about, I think. You'll be needing your emergency rations yet if you can't get back down again.'

'Well, come on then,' Bill Cooper snapped irritably. 'Let's get it done!'

The procession of trucks and landrovers slithered off down the track towards the kraal.

* * *

Kosie wasn't sure what to do. He was cold with a fear he had never known before. He'd meddled in other people's business; bad business, without knowing what was really happening, and he'd been the one to trigger all of this off. He wished he was back in Durban. They were hard on the streets, all right, but not like they were up here! Somehow, he was sure, he would be able to find those kids, and if he did then it would be all right again. Wouldn't it? A right against a wrong. Hadn't he heard somewhere about a tooth for an eye, or something? Well this was his chance to make things right.

But how to find them? That was the thing. Think about what the other guy might do. Put yourself in his shoes. What Kosie would do, based on his vast experience of comics, would be to climb up to a cave somewhere, lie low until all the fuss had died down, and then escape to a civilized place; like Durban. So all he had to do was find the cave, and there they would be.

When the truck he was hiding in skidded to a halt in front of Mubi's hut, Kosie slipped over the tailgate and made his way in the only sensible direction; up.

14

It was so dark. Mponyane was afraid of darkness because then he lost his one window onto the world. The lightning helped, but the flashes were so strong, blue-white across the eyes, that they blinded him and there were only a few seconds when he could see where he was. It was too late to turn back. Mponyane had led them upwards to the place where he thought the cave might be, but somewhere along the path he lost his sense of direction and now he didn't know where he was. Another flash exposed the rocks and stones around them, but he didn't recognize anything. Surely, if you did a right thing, a good thing, it would turn out well in the end? Baba would come for them, or Kra. Somebody would come.

They toiled up and up. Fan's face was very still and tired now. He didn't seem to question Mponyane's decisions, but just kept on climbing. They tried to shelter once under an overhanging rock, but the rain blasted in under it anyway and they became cold when they stopped moving. Fan was so wet that they might as well have thrown the raincoat away.

To keep himself cheerful, Mponyane thought about the place that they would find. It would be their own place where nobody would bother them, and once they had planted a few vegetables and built a hut, they would send for Baba and Kra and Cecy and they would all live together and nobody would hurt them.

Up and up they went. Mponyane slipped on a wet rock and slithered back down the path, but Fan managed to pull him up again, and he wasn't hurt much, just a few grazes. It was just a matter of keeping going; keeping on.

Bill Cooper was becoming increasingly disturbed. He'd hoped that the Saundersons would just leave, go away, let him get on with his life, but they persisted in battling against all odds on that stupid farm that never seemed to harvest any crops. Now they were all, together and separately, lost on the mountain in the worst storm in years. They were a damn nuisance.

It wasn't *his* fault – well not really. He'd never meant to keep the money; it was just temporary until he'd settled with the bank and the man from the casino who said he had to have the money now, or else. 'Or else what?' Bill had wondered, but he hadn't asked. OK, he did feel bad about the whole thing, quite a bit bad, as a matter of fact, but it's a wicked world. It had been a case of himself, or Saunderson – and that wasn't much of a choice, was it? Not with George still at 'varsity and Marcia's wedding to pay for. And it wasn't as if he hadn't worked for it. One mistake, that was all, one stupid mistake – and there had been the money in the Safety Fund just asking him to take it.

Bloody rain. He tramped on the heels of Paul Ross, who was ahead of him in the mud, and mumbled an apology. He supposed it was about time for him to get everyone motivated. None of the others would do it – or at least not while he was there. It had been that way right from about Standard One.

'What shall we play now, Bill?' and he had decided. 'Where shall we go now, Bill?' and he'd told them.

It was what power was all about, but it was a responsibility as well.

He supposed that, now he came to think of it, that was the thing he had least wanted to lose; the respect of the others, the admiration, the position. That was what had kept him from speaking up when Etienne Saunderson was accused of taking the money. He'd tried once or twice, on that terrible afternoon after the accident when accusations had been flying, but his voice hadn't wanted to say the words, and he'd remained silent. Even now he sometimes got the ridiculous urge to stop the Board Meeting or whatever and announce calmly, 'I took the money from the Safety Fund.' He thought about it a lot, especially at night, and he heard the words constantly in his mind. 'I took the money from the Safety Fund.'

He sighed heavily. This wouldn't get those kids found.

'Right chaps, I'll check this gully here, you lot split up at the fork in the path we saw on the map. Meet back here in twenty minutes – no more.'

In the wavering light from the helmet, rocks and stones glimmered in the driving wet. It was slippery underfoot, but the tough mining boots helped. He looked up at an eternity of mud and stone, sighed again, and started the climb.

Mponyane was becoming more and more disorientated. It was the flashing. He didn't like it. Everything became distorted and unreal and he needed, now more than ever, to *see* things. Sadness spread over him like Fan's wet coat, dragging him down. It came from inside and could not be stopped so that he thought it was pulling him away from what was real and understandable.

'Can we go home now?' Fan asked in a small voice,

forgetting that Mponyane couldn't hear. 'I'm frightened. I want to go back to Mom.'

A lurid slash of lightning lit his face. Mouth movements, mouth movements again; the secret code.

Suddenly inside Mponyane was an anger that threatened to choke him. Mouth movements! Mouth movements! Mouth movements! He wanted to have them as well. Why couldn't he have them? He picked up a stone that lay on the path and flung it with all his strength against the wall of rock that surrounded them, but even the sound of his stone was swallowed and drowned in the thunder that beat against Fan's ear, so that still Mponyane had no voice.

Frank was crying in earnest now. 'I'm frightened Mponyane! Take me home!'

Mponyane sagged against the rock. He was too sad to go on. He would lie here until day came, or the storm finished, or the rain stopped and then he would go back to the place of the people who weren't living somewhere else, and he would stay there with Mubi until he was old as well.

But the water came first.

High in the mountains where the rain had first begun, were rivers, and rivers, of water and mud that hurtled down towards the valley where the people were, and the farms, and the animals. Mponyane lifted his head in despair and saw it come, and he took Fan, who was crying still, and threw him with a strength that he did not really have, up onto the boulder that towered behind him.

And then there was black world where there was nothing, a deep and cold place where it did not matter that Mponyane could not hear, because there was no sound except the rushing and the rushing of the water, and no one spoke.

* * *

Kosie brought Frank down, a quiet, chastened Kosie who said that the black boy ought to have a medal. He'd seen it all, how Mponyane had saved Frank's life.

'It was the bravest thing I ever saw,' said Kosie, who had never seen anything brave at all in all his short and vicious life. And then he asked to be taken to Mrs Ross, who was his friend, and she was there because she had begged a lift with the police bakkie when the men from the station had come to join the search. They sat together in the Van Niekerk's kitchen and did not speak very much, but Kosie felt safe for the first time ever.

And the men brought Bill Cooper down as well, battered and bruised, half drowned and suffering from concussion. But he was quite lucid, taking control of everything as he always had done, asking for Jean Saunderson and her daughter to be brought to him as soon as they were found. And when they were brought he had no difficulty at all in saying the words he wanted to say, even though Sergeant Brand and half the men from the rescue team were standing listening.

'I took the money from the Safety Fund.'

Kra's words:

We went to the place, Etienne and Cecily and Frank and I, when the memory of the storm was a red scar on the earth and the sky was calm and still. We sat where we could look out over the valley, at peace below us, green, green after the rain. The children were quiet and I knew they were thinking of Mponyane. There were flowers, small white ones with dark green leaves. I did not know their name. It was hard to imagine that the water had torn this scene apart, only a few weeks before. It was hard to remember that Mponyane was gone.

Over the soft grass, a cloud of yellow butterflies danced; and were free.